Earthbound Wings

ReGina Welling

Earthbound Wings

Copyright © 2016 by ReGina Welling

ISBN- 978-1539396055

ISBN- 1539396053

Cover art by: L. Vryhof

Interior design by: L, Vryhof

www.reginawelling.com

First Edition

Printed in the U.S.A.

Table of Contents

Prologue..5

Chapter 1..7

Chapter 2..14

Chapter 3..16

Chapter 4..22

Chapter 5..33

Chapter 6..45

Chapter 7..55

Chapter 8..59

Chapter 9..63

Chapter 10..63

Chapter 11..79

Chapter 12..87

Chapter 13..87

Chapter 14..94

Chapter 15..117

Chapter 16..122

Chapter 17..136

Chapter 18..141

Chapter 19..149

Chapter 20..149

Chapter 21..166

Chapter 22..175

Chapter 23..182

Chapter 24..190

Epilogue..190

Dedication

This book is dedicated to all of my angels, but to one in particular.

To the only person from whom I would accept being called Pond Scum and laugh about it.

Love you, miss you, Kathleen.

Prologue

The odor of spoiled food mingled with something acrid enough to set camp in the back of my throat like a squatting demon pulled me back from gray nothing to frowning awareness. Cracking an eye open just far enough to take in my surroundings made the world spin with sickening force.

Dim shadows and brick walls shivered into focus, then out again as I breathed into the moist heat weighing heavy against my body. More minutes passed before my eyelids fluttered open again.

A desultory breeze whirled tattered bits of paper into the corner across from where I huddled in the shadows of a loading dock beside a hulking metal dumpster. Horns blared in the street at the end of the alley that was currently providing my dirty but relatively safe haven.

It had happened again. Waking up in weird places was starting to become my thing.

I am the angel Galmadriel.

Sort of, anyway. It's complicated. One or two bad decisions, a stupid mistake, and the next thing I know I'm yanked out of heaven and shoved into a human body.

Don't get me wrong, I know I deserve what happened to me, it's just that with no better plan for my new mortal life, the Powers That Be have decided to turn me into some kind of spiritual bounty hunter—minus the bounty. At least that's how it worked on my first assignment. Maybe this one would be different. Probably not.

Heat shimmers teased a cloud of buzzing flies toward a sticky puddle on the ground while, ignoring a few muscles twinging in protest, I levered myself off the concrete ledge and landed on the pavement.

"Thanks for not dropping me into oncoming traffic again," I grumbled, in case anyone up there was listening. The council of angels in charge of assignments was a group of poker-faced sticklers for a series of protocols so strict it was impossible to know how many steps there were between them and the divine. One thing I did know was just how seriously they took the job of caring for the souls on this physical plane, and for the ones in transition to the place I had recently called home.

Heaven, Earth, Valhalla, Olympus. Worlds within worlds—each considered both a myth and a reality depending on who you ask—exist alongside scores of realms in a honeycomb of darkness and light. Take a poll among the beings of each world and most will insist theirs is the more important, the ultimate one. Yet, there are those who haunt the fringes, who brave temptation and preying darkness to glimpse the glories and horrors of legend. Witches, the fair folk, ghouls that feed upon blood, or flesh, or spirit, and even angels like me walk in the gray places where shadow meets light, and balance is the only thing holding back chaos.

I am the angel Galmadriel, yet I am also the human known as Adriel. I live between worlds. I am earthbound.

Chapter 1

A second gust of wind, this one slightly cooler than the last, carried with it another scent. Fresh blood has a metallic tang to it, and enough of it had spilled nearby that the smell lay strong and coppery on the air. Dreading what she would find, Adriel ignored the screaming instincts urging her to run the other way and hurried toward the source.

Three steps past the end of the dumpster she walked right through a ghost. Little shivers of sensation ran across her skin, and not in a pleasant way. In her line of work, being scared of spirits makes about as much sense as hating the sight of blood and deciding to become a surgeon. You might be able to get the job done, but you'd never be really good at it. Adriel was really good at her job, so ghosts didn't bother her normally, but this experience had the element of surprise going for it.

During that one brief touch, everything the ghost had endured during her final moments transferred to Adriel in a rush of sensation and none of what she saw or felt was pretty. A black hood shadowed the upper part of her murderer's face, leaving only the glimpse of a stubbled chin to identify him by. Rough hands ripped at the girl's hair. Adriel felt it all, including the hot sting of the blade as it sank between the victim's ribs. And the long, slow slide of lifeblood pooling into a sticky mess beneath her. Right at the end, the girl had heard the voice of someone begging her not to die, then cursing himself for being too late.

7

So caught up was Adriel in the voyeuristic vision of the younger woman's death that she didn't see the man standing guard over the body. Or the seething blackness darker than a shadow reaching past him toward the spirit cowering against the bricks. In the split second before chaos broke loose, Adriel caught an impression of white blond hair spilling over broad shoulders and a red garment billowing around the man like a cape. Except no one wears capes anymore, right?

"Mine." The word hissed out of the dark mass in a gust of fetid breath.

"Never." The mysterious protector shouted as he gathered energy into a crackling ball of light and threw it at the shadowed figure. The smell of ozone hit Adriel just before a small blast of heated air tossed her hair across her face. Nothing but a haze of smoke remained.

"Eat fire, Jackwad. She's not for you." Blond-cape guy's voice sounded ragged from the force of his battle cry, and he pumped a fist in the air, then whirled to make sure his charge was safe. He took two steps before he noticed Adriel and she had to give him credit for how successfully he covered his surprise. His eyes, clear and crystal blue, roved over the former guardian angel from head to toe, searching for any evidence of her involvement in the crime.

Adriel's presence drew the crusader's focus so tightly he was looking the wrong way when the single wisp of darkness that had escaped being vanquished by his ball of light deepened to shadow and resolved itself again into something vaguely man-shaped. It rose up behind him so quickly there was no time for warning. Desperate to save him, Adriel's instincts took over and did something she had been unable to accomplish on her own for quite some time. With a whisper of sound and a flash of dazzling white, her wings flared out and folded over the man and the spirit.

Just in time, too.

8

The dark thing slammed up against pure, feathered light with a sound like a bug hitting a zapper—if the bug was the size of a car, and the zapper was the size of a house. It had about the same effect, too. Little flecks of burnt shadow shot up, then fell back to earth like black snow, each flake disappearing before hitting the ground. Several buzzing seconds passed before Adriel could gather her senses enough to realize the blue-eyed man was plastered against the front of her. Up close and personal. It was the first time she had been able to exert any control over her wings since becoming earthbound.

Half a second later, I had to amend that thought. No one was in control of her wings—particularly not her. All efforts to fold them away failed, and the harder she tried the more they fouled against the close confines of the narrow alleyway. Physical body, physical wings. Huge ones. Great. Just what she needed at that particular moment.

"We have to get out of here unless you want to explain this," the protector of innocent ghosts gestured to encompass the area around himself: dead woman on the ground; bits of shadow still floating lazily in the air; the foul, brimstone smell of burnt darkspawn so strong it was an almost visible haze. "There's not much time." The distant wail of sirens bore out his claim.

"Did you kill her?"

"No, I didn't kill her. Look, not a drop of blood on me." The hands he held up were clean, and Adriel chose to believe him. "But we need to go. Right now!"

"I can't. My wings are stuck open."

"Put them around me again." When she didn't immediately respond to his arrogant order, he gestured impatiently and said, "Hurry up." He stepped close enough to press against her again and she had no choice but to ignore the

9

way her pulse leapt and her breath shortened. "Now," his voice thundered in her ear, and she did as he asked. It might have been the reaction to his tone, or that she had stopped actively struggling with them, but the white feathers fell into place without a fight.

All Adriel felt was a little tug in her belly—maybe a ripple of motion—and then everything went still and quiet.

"You can let go now. We're safe." The man treated Adriel to a warm, slightly crooked smile that set her nerves tingling and made her stumble away from him with all the grace of a newborn giraffe. The only bright spot in all the awkwardness was when, because she wasn't thinking about them, her wings folded back effortlessly and vanished from sight. Guilt for having shown them to a mortal played around the edges of Adriel's thoughts, but she rationalized it away since the man had already shown he was more than merely human.

"My name is Adriel." She held out her hand for the preferred greeting, but he ignored it.

"Leith. And I know who you are. Tell me you brought the dead girl along." He glanced behind Adriel as though she might be hiding the errant spirit somewhere behind her body.

"Technically it was you who brought us to…where are we?" A dozen pines circled the clearing where they stood, the previous year's spills creating a rust-colored carpet that gave off a pungent, earthy smell. A ring of stones marked a second circle inside the larger one. This was a place of power. His place, if Adriel wasn't mistaken.

Leith ignored the question. "Tell me you didn't lose the girl's shade. If she's not with you, we'll have to go back for her." He paced a few steps before turning his face back toward Adriel impatiently. Tight leather pants molded over his lower body, leaving very little to the imagination below a white shirt with puffy sleeves. Was he going for pirate or handsome prince? Or was this the preferred look for arrogant jerks this year?

"No one wears capes anymore. Or is there a runway somewhere missing its model?" That came out snarkier than Adriel normally spoke.

"I know you did your best back there, but I had things under control until you stuck your nose in where it didn't belong." He, on the other hand, totally meant to be that condescending.

"Under control? Another ten seconds and you would have been spook kibble, Obi Wan."

Centuries of watching over humans hadn't given Adriel a tenth of the perspective she'd gotten in the past couple of months living as one of them. She now understood why heightened emotions led people to treat each other badly sometimes—the irrational fire that burned hot in the belly and turned the brain to thoughts of wanton destruction. It's a fact, angels get mad, but it takes a lot more than being treated to a bit of attitude to get one riled up to the point of unleashing sudden wrath upon the world. Usually.

Therefore, Adriel concluded that since her personal wrath-o-meter was now calibrated to a matter of small degrees, the extreme anger response must come from something bred into the flesh or bone. Leith pushed it to the redline with no more effort than it took to breathe. Hot words gushed against her tongue, so it was a struggle to speak in a mild tone, "Explaining your motives would go a long way toward enlisting my help."

The girl must have crossed over. Somewhere between the time when Adriel's wings closed over the three of them and when the feathery whiteness had turned into a demon zapper, she remembered hearing the girl's spirit say eek, and she thought she might have seen a flash of leg racing away toward white mist backlit by a bright light.

"Look, Adriel, the world is going to hell, in case you missed it, and I don't have time for the tea and cookies version. I'll drop you somewhere safe before I get back to the business of aiding defenseless spirits against the darkness." Leith's gaze measured the former angel; the sneer on his lips indicated she had been found wanting.

Hot fury must have triggered the center of Adriel's power because she felt it flare to life in a prickling haze of energy. It felt good, strong, and right. The snotty jerk's eyes went wide when he felt the electric heat of it slide over his skin, and to his credit, Leith paled a little at the sensation. Adam's apple bobbing as he swallowed, he held up a hand. "Okay, okay. Take it down a notch. No offense, but I heard you wouldn't be much of a player in your current condition." His eyes raked over her a second time while his words made Adriel sound like an invalid. It rankled.

She bit down on a quick retort and channeled the extra energy back into the seat of all power. It went smoothly, which sparked the hope that she might get beyond the stage of merely being reconnected to her abilities and find herself in control of them again soon. Instinct is good, and it had saved her—them—today, but she preferred predictability to this feeling of riding the edge.

Needing a minute to think, Adriel stalked to the edge of the inner circle where a fine sense of protection buzzed through the energy signature, along with something more. Curious, she lifted a hand to test the swirling current. Behind her, Leith's breath whistled on a sharp intake. The merest brush across the curtain of his will gave her a better sense of the intention behind it, and she dropped her head back to let the sensations come.

12

Flaming red curls slithered down her proud back as a complex series of emotions washed over and through Adriel. Helplessness, burning anger, determination to protect the innocent. She needed more, and so she ruthlessly thrust both hands into the energy field and sifted through it to find the deepest truth: utter certainty that this work would eventually cost him his life, and an unfailing resolution to continue on despite the consequences. Darned if she didn't find him admirable. Pigheaded, stubborn, and reckless, but admirable.

Oh, and attractive. Let's not gloss over that.

"I think she crossed over right before..." And the world went black. Again.

Chapter 2

For the second time in what she hoped was the same day, Adriel woke up in an alley. What was that saying people used? The one that had made no sense to her until she'd gained a human body. Déjà vu all over again. Given the chance to make a list of wishes, not being bandied around in space without warning or prior consent would be right up there in her top three.

No coppery scent of fresh blood mixed with the stench of hot garbage, so at least that was different this time. Looking around at the brick walls, sharply scented puddles leaking from the trash bins, and broken pallets that littered the narrow space, Adriel concluded one city alley looked much like another. Great, she thought, with all the chaos, she'd been a little too busy that first time to memorize the exact layout and now she had no idea if she had landed in the same alley or even the same city.

A moment spent in the attempt to orient herself to place and time only got half the job done. Same city, different alley. An angel always knows where and when she is, an angel in a human body has no such certainty. If her locational senses were correct, leaving this spot and traveling four blocks east would take Adriel to the park where her friend Pam ran the mobile part of her bakery out of the back of a food truck. Place was the easy part, how long had passed since her first visit, or since leaving Leith's clearing was anyone's guess.

Tall walls on either side of her blocked out enough sunlight to cast the alley into partial shade, though with the shade came no sense of coolness. The narrow city canyon was sticky, dank, and redolent with dumpster odors. Though Adriel could see vehicles and foot traffic passing outside, the small space between two buildings felt as remote as a desert oasis. Wobbling to her feet, Adriel began to pick her way toward the mouth of the alley and civilization.

She managed fewer than five careful steps when she sensed a disruption in the energy around her. Something was coming in fast.

Chapter 3

Slapping a faerie out of the air is considered impolite if she is feeling generous, and a grave insult any other time—but when said faerie is about the size of a dragonfly and only inches from getting tangled in your hair, these things happen. The tiny creature burned the air with a trail of curse words that flowed along behind her as she spun out of control. The force of her ire left an arch of sparkling motes that made Adriel think of wisps of smoke and put the image of an angry cartoon character into her head. She chastised herself for having watched too much TV during her last assignment. The sound of the thud when the winged faerie hit the ground was disproportionately loud enough to make Adriel clap her hands over her ears.

"Sorry." When the echo of the impact died down, Adriel infused the word with heartfelt emotion and still knew it came out sounding lame. Light flared behind three or four upended wooden pallets where the indignant Fae had crashed, and while the earthbound angel watched in fascination, the faerie's insect-sized figure grew to her full height. On the tall side herself, Adriel estimated the Fae woman topped her by several inches. "I didn't mean to..."

"Save it." Cool and collected now, the faerie twitched a lock of hair the color of Caribbean water back into place. Her hand was tipped with nails that had a glittering finish so clear they resembled mirrored puddles and reflected every filthy detail of the narrow alley. "Follow me." A swirl of dark blue material and a flash of pale flesh moved in a blur toward the mouth of the brick-sided city path before Adriel had time for a longer look.

Resentful of the order, Adriel stood her ground.

"I said follow me." The command fell through the air like the notes from a gong, sparking an impulse from the half of Adriel anchored to flesh and bone. She wanted to follow the creature before her—was nearly compelled to do so—and yet, the angel's feet remained firmly planted. Angel trumps faerie in the compel-by-supernatural-means department. Every single time.

A little flick of Adriel's iron will and the command cease blew the faerie's water-colored hair back into disarray.

"Let's not get into a contest over which one of us has the bigger…stick." The faerie held up a hand. "I'm Evian." Irises, the color of a white-capped wave, surrounded luminous black pupils in eyes narrowed to convey her annoyance over having to provide even that brief explanation. "You want to help Julius, don't you?"

His name commanded Adriel's full attention.

Julius was her responsibility—a guardian angel in training under Adriel's care—and if she took time to think about it, he was the direct reason for her current earthbound predicament. Loathe to let his earthly fortune go undiscovered, Julius had chosen not to cross over after death.

It happens more often than you think.

Spirits remain anchored to this plane for many reasons, most of them benign. Some stay thinking they will find a way to avenge a perceived wrong. That motivation alone is enough to provide a tenuous connection with the evil forces that inhabit the dark realms and can set an otherwise well-meaning ghost on the path toward becoming something else: Ghoul,

Earthwalker, or some other form of darkspawn. Few ever make it that far; it takes an inordinate amount of determination and a truly blackened soul to descend to darkness, which means there are a lot of misguided spirits like Julius wandering the earth.

When an Earthwalker takes a human vessel, the human dies. That's how it has always been—until recently, anyway. As far as Adriel knew, she was the only angel ever to save a human vessel. More or less, anyway. Years of bilking the elderly out of their life savings had done plenty to blacken the soul of Logan Ellis long before the Earthwalker got hold of him. If not for the faith of four unique women, the remaining shred of decency Logan had buried deep inside might never have been strong enough to let him survive. Adriel could only hope the man would find atonement behind prison walls as he served his sentence.

Julius, his own soul in no danger of becoming dark, had still managed to inadvertently serve as a conduit between Billy the Earthwalker and Logan, the ex-fiancé of his own great-granddaughter, Julie Hayward-Kingsley. The situation had spun out of control long before one of Adriel's charges, an aura reader named Amethyst, stepped into the fray to help Julie and, by extension, dragged her guardian angel into the escalating problem. By the time the dust cleared on that debacle, Logan was saved and the demon, Billy, had been banished back to the darkness. But the error in judgment had also rendered Adriel earthbound and changed everything in her world.

Now Julius was in trouble—most likely because Adriel's lack of foresight—and she felt duty-bound to save him. If this faerie could help, not even the legends warning against following any of the fair folk back to their homes would stop Adriel from going along to find out.

"Evian? Like the bottled water?" Adriel didn't mean it to come out all snarky like that. Good thing Evian was a water worker and not a creature of fire given the scorching look she tossed over her shoulder. Going up in flames wasn't the most auspicious way for Adriel to regain her angelhood.

"I vow to provide you safe passage to and from our destination. Now, do you want to help Julius or not?" She did, so Adriel stopped talking and walked alongside the faerie, their long strides eating up the blocks between downtown and Tidewell Park. Halfway there, two things occurred to Adriel. First, that this was the second time today a map had formed in her head to provide a current position and a likely destination. An angel ability she thought she had lost. And second, no one was paying any attention to the pair of striking women as they strode down the street. At all.

Odd. Now that Adriel was human, more or less, she expected to blend in somewhat, but Evian stood out like a poppy in a field of dandelions. She must be casting a glamour to hide her true appearance. Following that thought to its logical conclusion, if Evian's efforts didn't work on Adriel, she must have regained some of her inherent angel powers— like the ability to pierce veils. Not as handy as being able to move through time and space, but better than nothing.

"Not very chatty, are you?" Adriel was saved from hearing what would probably be a scathing retort when a warbling noise rose from her pocket. Reaching in, she pulled out the cell phone acquired during her last assignment. The thing should have been all but dead given whatever caused her to have a negative effect on electronics since Adriel had gained a physical body. Miraculously, it appeared to be in perfect working order. Amethyst's name popped on the display along with the date.

Two weeks had passed while Adriel was...well, she wasn't sure where she had been or why she had no memory of where she went between assignments. Muttering a request for forgiveness, Adriel pressed ignore and pulled up the call log. Missed calls from Amethyst and the others—at least one from each of them for every day since she had been gone marched down the screen. Scrolling back, Adriel saw that Pam Allen's number showed up for a few days, then petered out. Maybe that was for the best since those who were behind Adriel's current assignment hadn't left time enough to say goodbye to the woman who had both her former employer and her first assignment as an earthbound angel. Oh, who was she kidding? Pam had gone beyond being a mere assignment and become a friend.

A yellow banner popped up over the top of the call log to remind Adriel the only way she would hear her messages was if she set up voice mail. That, too, would have to wait until after Evian finally decided to spill the beans about Julius. Adriel stuffed the phone back into her pocket. Figuring out the reason behind her changing effect on electronics would have to go on the To Do list.

Heat spiraled up from the dark pavement like impending doom without the slightest breath of a breeze to bring relief. Complaining about the heat, while tempting, wouldn't bring relief. Brick and steel speared skyward on either side, turning the street into a man-made canyon with traffic running like a river between its walls.

There was no need for a mirror to tell Adriel she looked like a wilted flower. Pale skin prone to freckling reddened quickly under even the gentlest rays, and today the sun was blazing down like an angry god. Hair, the color of autumn leaves, ran in tangled curls down her back and plastered itself against her scalp. Evian, blast her, looked fresh as a water lily. That alone was enough to make Adriel cranky.

It took less than half an hour and felt like double that time before Evian turned into the space between the stone pillars that served as a gateway to the park. Intricately carved gargoyles leered down from the top of each column, their faces seeming creepily real despite the bas-relief.

Leading her largely unwilling guest toward the grassy banks of the bay lining the far edge of Tidewell Park, Evian used a quick nod of her head to indicate Adriel should follow her as she stepped into the water. Green scum ringed the shoreline and floated greasily among a patch of reeds as the faerie's passage through cloudy water released the scent of long-dead fish and mud.

"What are you doing?" Adriel planted her feet at the water's edge. She was not going to wade through that muck.

"We need to speak privately. This is the place where I have the most control. It's my element. Are you going to stand there all day or follow me and help Julius?" Evian moved the fingers of her right hand through a complicated gesture that made Adriel shiver when it triggered a feeling like cobwebs settling over her skin. Evian waited, impatience written in the tightness of her shoulders and the tilt of her head.

"I'm coming." Thinking the water would be cool, Adriel wrinkled her nose and took a step into the wetness. To her utter shock, the liquid flowed around her foot, which remained completely dry. "Nice trick, but you know I can't breathe under water, right?"

The tiniest smile played around Evian's mouth. "Thanks for stating the obvious. Will you come? I promised you safe passage, remember?"

A promise from a Fae was solid as gold, so Adriel walked willingly into the murky depths of the bay.

Chapter 4

When the water closed over her head, Adriel experienced a momentary freakout, but since Evian's back was to her, hoped the faerie hadn't witnessed the utter loss of cool. Evian's spell worked like a charm, or maybe it was a charm, who knew? Call it whatever you want, it let Adriel breathe under water without drowning. Pretty nifty.

Once the panic subsided, Adriel started noticing things. Like the way Evian's body gave off light in a radius of about six yards. And the way the silt and mud under their feet turned solid enough to support their weight without letting their feet sink into the squelching depths. The pair passed several rusting hulks of old cars and trucks that had no business being there, and Adriel spared a passing thought for whatever catastrophe had sent them into the watery depths.

Everything around her undulated to the beat of a slow rhythm that even their passing couldn't completely alter. The dance of the sea was a waltz in three:four time.

Just about the time when Adriel began wondering if she would be forced to walk forever, Evian passed through an archway built from a pair of airplane wings jammed into the sea floor and topped by the overturned hull of a boat with its name emblazoned upon the side, *Ship of Fools.*

How appropriate.

Evian's lair would have been the perfect set for a live-action retelling of Disney's The Little Mermaid. It was so true to form a singing crab might float by at any second. Discarded items lay on shelves formed from rocks and debris. A brass teapot, a puddle of gold and silver chains, and a large bucket filled with rusting guns rested among the detritus.

"Sit." Ever the queen of brevity, Evian led the way to a pair of paint-flaked bistro chairs, and prepared—Adriel hoped—to elaborate on why she felt it necessary to go to such lengths to have a private conversation. "We're just waiting for my sisters to get here. Shouldn't be long. In the meantime, tell me how this," a mirror-tipped hand waved to indicate Adriel's fleshly body, "happened."

Really? Now she wanted to chat? Adriel shot Evian a raised eyebrow.

"Earthwalker. Battle. Error in judgment. Earthbound." The former angel nutshelled it for the water Fae.

Surprisingly, Evian threw back her head and laughed. "You are everything I had hoped you would be."

"Is that so?" Wondering how Evian could possibly have formed a set of perceptions about someone she'd yet to meet, Adriel was about to demand an explanation when a disturbance overhead drew her attention. A fireball, of all things, arced through the water on a collision course for the sitting area. Instinct sent Adriel diving for cover under the table while Evian's silvery laugh pealed out above her head.

The flaking lattice of a metal chair back only partially obscured Adriel's vision as the fireball resolved itself into another female figure.

"Adriel, this is my sister, Soleil."

Attempting to rise with some semblance of dignity and struggling with the effort, Adriel scrambled out from under the table. Soleil was a vision of opposites compared to her sister.

A short cap of disordered hair the color of glowing embers set off a pair of wide, dark eyes in a narrow face of palest ivory. Her lips were black as coal.

"What do you think? Can she handle it? Is she as good as we hoped?" Soleil ignored the newcomer to ask Evian the questions. Angry heat prickled over Adriel's face.

"You can see me, right? I'm standing right here." Courtesy between species of supernatural beings aside, she'd had just about enough of this. Drawing herself up to full height, she let her voice thunder with power. "Stop wasting my time."

The command affected the pair of them, but not in any expected way. Wide smiles creased their faces, and one of the sisters let out a giggle. "I guess that's as good an answer as any. Be calm, Adriel. Terra should be here any second, and then all will be revealed." Soleil assured while Adriel silently named the stars until she had herself under control. Very little aggravated her nerves more than being ordered to remain calm. "Julius said you were a badass."

"If anything happens to Julius while I'm fooling around with this underwater coffee klatch, rest assured, I will show you exactly how bad my ass can be." Another giggle did nothing to help my mood, and neither did the effort it took to bypass the filters the Powers had installed to render angels incapable of uttering certain words. It seemed to Adriel as if free will should have come along with her conversion to humanity.

The temptation to storm out of there was great, but she estimated her chances of drowning before she could get to the surface to be somewhere above fifty percent. In full angel form, she could have walked for miles underwater without needing a protective charm. Now Adriel wouldn't bet her left shoe on being able to pull it off. Plus, she burned to know what the sisters could tell her about Julius, so she bit her tongue and waited in seething silence for Terra to show up.

Blessedly, it didn't take long. A whirlpool of mud bubbled up from the mucky seabed. Layer upon layer of wet soil and silt built into the form of a lushly endowed woman. Mahogany hair streaked in shades of earth tones swirled around a stunning face. Lips of apple red smiled below eyes the color of pink marble, and Terra's skin held the ripe blush of a peach.

Evian pulled two more chairs from some hidden alcove and got down to the business at hand. Guardian angels and faeries don't normally spend a lot of time together since they run in entirely different circles, plus there's that whole misconception that all Fae are evil and angels are sworn to fight them. The truth is nothing is ever entirely black or white, particularly not an entire race.

As some form of a cosmic joke, Julius had been assigned to Adriel to serve in both the capacity of her guardian angel and her trainee. She found it galling to be on the receiving end of the work she had spent lifetimes perfecting.

Worse, it wasn't only Julius, either. Along with him had come Adriel's second trainee, Estelle. The second half of the unholy team who, upon her death, had been recruited by Julius to turn ghost in order to help their granddaughter find a hidden inheritance. Neither one had foreseen the harsh consequences of their decision to remain in limbo in the spirit world.

"You seem to know a lot about Julius, but have any of you been in contact with Estelle?" Adriel hoped she wasn't in trouble, too. Dealing with two green angels at the same time felt a lot like herding kittens. Kittens with highly developed senses of mischief and altogether too much raw power.

"She'll be along soon, I'm sure." Terra's voice was earthy like the rest of her. "She's up to speed on the situation."

"So I'm the only one in the dark?" Mounting frustration bolstered what kinetic energy Adriel still had at her command. "My patience is coming to an end, so either get on with it or let me go." Shock waves rippled through Evian's grotto, tipped a few of her haphazardly ordered piles off the makeshift shelves.

"The little guardian has untapped potential." Admiration colored Soleil's tone. "It will be a few days more before Julius is beyond saving. He's wily, that one. If I didn't know better, I'd say he was Fae-touched."

The urge to war must be coded somewhere in human flesh because Adriel couldn't remember ever being tempted to commit murder prior to taking her place among the living. "Where is Julius?" she ground the words out from between clenched teeth.

"Taken prisoner by one of your own."

Adriel knew exactly who Evian meant, and faerie's dry tone honed the edge of the earthbound angel's temper to a point sharp enough to stab.

"Malachiel." Adriel spit the name like a forbidden curse word.

"Yes. He calls himself Blackwing now, and his firsthand knowledge of angel ways makes him doubly dangerous. It was he who lured your compatriot to his doom."

"His doom?" Heart lurching in her chest, Adriel had to know. "You don't mean Julius is…tell me he is not among the fallen."

An undefinable look passed between the three faeries. "No, he still shines." Soleil sighed, and her expression turned thoughtful. "The fallen angel is only a symptom of the larger problem. Have you lost the ability to feel the subtle alterations in the balance between darkness and light? The underworlds have been rising in power."

26

"How long?" A feeling of foreboding threatened to steal Adriel's breath.

"A few months in mortal world time."

Just about the length of time since Adriel had become earthbound. Could this be her fault?

"It seems Julius blundered into the middle of a subtle bid for power and became an unwitting pawn in the war."

It was just like him to end up in the center of controversy.

"Tell me everything. Do you know where he is? I need to help him." Thinking not of her own redemption, Adriel focused only on the angel in trouble. Whatever it took to save him, she was prepared to do.

Another look passed between the Fae, and it was as though a veil fell away. "Julius insisted you could be trusted, but we needed to see for ourselves." Terra reached across the table to lay a warm hand on Adriel's chilled one; her touch grounded and comforted the earthbound angel while the three Fae described the events they felt signaled the beginning of a shift in the cosmic equilibrium.

None of what they had to say came as a shock to one who had witnessed more than a few power struggles in her infinite life.

Would it surprise you to know that the ultimate goal of evil is not to create some sort of apocalyptic event meant to turn the world black? Why? Because the universe and all the worlds require duality. Good and evil, light and dark, Seelie and Unseelie, on and off, in and out. An abundance of opposites.

Putting out the light does not mean the dark will rule; the end of duality would mean both will disappear into the vacuum and the world will cease to exist. It's impossible to rule a fallen world. What's more, if one world falls, the domino effect is likely to take the rest down, too, and it's hard to rule a world that no longer exists. Better to nudge the world toward gray than black.

Most denizens of the dark are not nihilists. But, within the flux state, there will always be room for power struggles meant to push the balance toward good or evil without passing the ultimate tipping point. A few more souls turning from the light in the human realm has repercussions everywhere, even among the Fae, where power and politics take the place of religion, and where right and wrong are only concepts, not laws.

Still, every millennium or so, some half-wit got the brilliant idea to flout the rules and spark an uprising. Nine times out of ten, it was a darkling. It was rare for a lightworker to go rogue and attempt to push humans toward the type of enlightenment that would cause harm. The last time it had happened, the city of Atlantis suffered catastrophic results.

"Another demon uprising." Adriel sighed. She'd been there and done that before.It never ended well for the idiot who set the whole thing in motion. "And Julius got caught up in it."

Luring Julius into harm's way had been all too easy. His highly developed instinct for justice during his human existence had, with angelhood, strengthened into what could become his biggest asset or his greatest downfall. With no more than a whisper in his ear that an innocent required assistance, he had walked into the trap willingly.

Half of Adriel reacted to this news with an all too human inclination for violence. If the hair-brained fool had been within arm's reach, she might have throttled him for overstepping his bounds and wandering off into avenging angel territory. Barely trained and greener than the seaweed currently swirling around her ankles, Julius would be lucky to last a week in the halls of vengeance. The other half of her admired his quick thinking and willingness to stand for the light. The arrogant twit could have asked for help, though. Isn't there a saying about learning from the mistakes of others?

"This time it's different. Whoever is behind the bid for control is mounting a subtle attack," Evian took up the narrative. "Yours isn't the only world in jeopardy for a change."

"Just imagine what would happen if the netherworlds in each realm pushed close to the edge of the darkest balance limit at the same time." Terra paused to let Adriel's imagination provide a visual. "It wouldn't be Armageddon, but it's as close as you're going to get to hell on Earth—and everywhere else."

Adriel pressed a hand against her forehead. Hard. Nothing stopped the headache which brought with it a healthy dose of guilt. Given the timing, this cosmic imbalance could have been brought on by the epic mistake she made when she partially demolished the rainbow bridge. The thought shoved the pain up past dull throb to pounding agony.

"Is that how you ended up involved? Aren't the Fae known for taking the neutral ground in these sorts of things?" *Even when it's your own people causing the problem.* Adriel left the last part unsaid. These Fae were making an effort to help, so throwing shade on them probably wasn't a good idea.

All three sets of eyes found someplace else to land that was as far away from meeting Adriel's as possible. Soleil shuffled her feet like a small child called to the principal's office, and quailed under the angle's best withering stare.

"Our sister Vaeta fell into the darkness almost a hundred human years ago."

"What does your sister have to do with Julius? And how did she *fall* into the darkness?" Adriel seized on the words, not for their ambiguous nature alone, but because the tone of Soleil's voice when she said them spoke volumes. "You think she went dark on purpose?"

The stricken look on the faerie's face told Adriel she'd hit on the heart of the matter. Tears with a flickering, fiery shine leaked from Soleil's eyes and turned to steam when they met water. On a sob, the fire faerie pushed away from the table, her passage freeing another flurry of rust-backed paint flakes from its metal surface. Terra cast a dirty look at Adriel, then rose and followed to soothe her sister while Evian remained seated.

"Vaeta is an airhead. Literally." Evian's face hardened. "It's her element almost as much as her nature. Air is easier to influence than earth, fire, or water. All it took was one blowhard whispering in her ear to push her off course."

"Don't talk about her like that." When Soleil's tone turned hot, the temperature of the water rose a degree or two. "She wasn't an airhead."

"Dial it back, Sunspot, you'll start steaming up the place."

"Don't tell me what to do, Pond Scum." Another degree of heat.

"Enough, you two." Terra eyed her sisters sternly.

"Back off. Being an Earth Mother doesn't make you mine." Soleil retorted, but the temperature dropped back to normal. The smug smile Terra turned Adriel's way went unnoticed by her sisters.

"I take it Vaeta had something to do with Julius' abduction?" I directed my question to Evian.

"According to him, she was the bait." She spat the words like bitter venom. "In her airy faerie form she resembles a ghost, so all she had to do was let him think she was a lost spirit trying to find her way home. Malachiel used some trick to make himself appear light again, then posed as an authority figure and convinced Julius this was a side mission that required him to take on physical form. Vaeta lured him into one of few places on this plane where he could be physically trapped."

"But why? What could he possibly gain from taking a newly minted guardian? Julius is still in training." *Lousy training with a not-quite angel,* Adriel thought. *Clearly I was not the right person or the right angel for the job.*

Terra answered, "That's the big mystery. We have some theories, but you aren't going to like them." She paused, and Adriel gestured for her to continue. "We think Darkwing—Malachiel—is working for someone else. Maybe a higher demon, or another faction. Either way, we get the impression he's nothing more than a minion."

Adriel suffered an instant mental image of Malachiel as one of those little yellow bean-looking characters with blue pants and big eyes. She had to hold back a snort.

What slipped out was a sigh. "Mal hates me for something I don't even remember doing. Are you certain this isn't his way of getting revenge on me?"

"The cherry on the sundae maybe, but we think not." Coming from Terra, the denial lifted some of the burden from Adriel's shoulders, but added almost the same weight back, because now she had less to go on in figuring out Mal's motives.

"Your situation is…" Terra paused to search for a word, "…unique. A situation that would have made you the perfect candidate for being captured if not for your level of experience. Correct me if I'm wrong, but you have always been an angel unlike Julius and Estelle, who were elevated to that status." Adriel nodded while wondering where the faerie had gotten her information.

"Julius made it all too easy, didn't he? They dangled the bait, and he didn't have the wisdom to see through to the truth." The sorrow that welled up from Adriel's soul and the look in Terra's eyes was all the answer needed.

"If there had been more time, we think Darkwing might have taken more time in trying to turn your guardian using subtler methods."

"Temptation and brainwashing? It would never have worked. Even a newbie like Julius would have seen right through Malachiel; subtle is not his specialty." Then the deeper realization set in. "You think they're going to force Julius into darkness?"

"What would happen if an Earthwalker took an angel by force? One who had not chosen the darkness; one who had not fallen. Would a possessed, but upright angel be able to carry the stained soul back to your home?"

A chilling theory.

"I'd like to see one try something that epically stupid. There has to be a seed of darkness already present for the Earthwalker to feed on. Only an angel who had chosen to fall would be ripe for the planting. Using force would be suicide. With fireworks and a candy apple."

"Right." Terra shook her head like Adriel had said something stupid and then waited for the light to dawn on her. When it did, the bottom dropped out of Adriel's world.

Chapter 5

"Julius isn't the intended victim, is he? He's only the bait. I'm the one they're after."

It made perfect sense that both a kernel of darkness and one of light rested within Adriel's human body. All mortals carry both. Still, what would be the point? If the goal is to infiltrate her heavenly home, she explained to the faeries, she was the last person an Earthwalker would choose for a vessel because home was the one place, ironically, where Adriel wasn't allowed to go.

"With you as the target, a whole other set of possible motives springs to mind," Evian mused. "A coup to take over the realm of light, one of the fallen is trying to get back home and that's just for starters. There could be someone crazy enough to want the end of all things. Seems like you should already have some idea who would have the biggest ax to grind. Angels have perfect recall, right?

The easy answer was yes, which would be the technically correct answer. Angels *do* have perfect recall. Adriel, however, did not. Three months had passed between the time she walked out the front door of Hayward House after the rainbow bridge debacle and when she reappeared in front of a speeding food truck. Three months she could not account for, and another two weeks had been lost before she landed in that alley today.

Adriel wanted to give Evian the easy answer, but her history of telling lies—even the ones that were technically truths—made the prospect iffy at best.

Soleil saved her from having to test those particular waters by asking an even more awkward question, "What are you really? Half an angel? A quarter?" she circled and appraised with the hint of a sneer playing about her mouth. That the answer was more complicated than a mere matter of degrees was something Adriel preferred to keep to herself, but the question had been asked, and the onus upon all angels forced an answer. The truth.

"I honestly don't know. By the most convenient definitions, you would consider me fully human. I require food and rest. I have," a mild shudder ran through Adriel with this admission, "bodily functions that I must attend to on a regular basis. If you cut me, I will bleed, and if I bleed enough, I will die like any other mortal." So far she Adriel knew, she spoke truly.

"So, hardly any angel at all?" Soleil's posture changed. Her shoulders dropped as if a heavy weight had just fallen on them.

"Enough." Pushing away from the table, Adriel took a deep breath, said a prayer that felt like it got through, and drew on the seat of all power. A fifty-fifty gamble that worked. The light of creation flowed into her soul with a rush. Everything else fell away—the sisters, her worries, the pain of feeling outcast—as she let the light fill her with purity and reveled in the way it burned away her doubts if only for the briefest of moments.

In a single movement, the three faeries stood and moved back a few steps from the table, as if the shining light was too bright for them at close range.

Mouth gaping open, Soleil's eyes reflected back to Adriel her true form. Hair whiter than snow fell like rain around wide shoulders to brush gently over the feathery light that made up glittering wings. Crystal green eyes stood out large in a face of exquisite pale beauty. Love for all the creatures of all the worlds swept away every vestige of fear or doubt in the same way her light-filled self had shed the flesh that anchored those emotions. In this place and in this time, she was the angel Galmadriel, a being born of the glory of creation, and nothing more. It felt amazing. It felt like home.

Ever so gradually, she let the power fade and exchanged it for the weight and doubt and pain of returning skin and bone and sinew. Flesh doused her light as surely as water eats flame. Adriel doubted if she could repeat the performance a second time. This had been an answer to prayer. Nothing more.

The feeling of being separated from home returned even stronger than before.

"Well, okay then." Terra nudged Soleil aside and returned to her seat. "That answers that, and now we know why you are the target." A shake of her head dispelled the last of the buzzing she undoubtedly felt in the presence of angelic grace. "The opportunity to corrupt an angel who has not chosen to fall is unprecedented."

"Mal wanted me to think kidnapping Julius was a personal vendetta. He wanted to add more fuel to the fire. Getting my emotions riled up makes me more vulnerable."

"From what Estelle has told us, he underestimated you once and it backfired on him." Terra's lips curved into a genuine smile that would terrify anyone who had never had contact with a delighted faerie before.

Leaning back in her chair, Adriel crossed her arms, and said, "There's a lot of that going around—underestimating me,

I mean." Without dimming her smile, Evian acknowledged the barb in those words with a nod of her head. "I trust you won't make the same mistake?"

"Your little guardians were right. I do like you." Evian laughed, though her eyes flicked toward her two sisters as they sat back down at the table.

"When did you meet Estelle?" Had her second trainee had been keeping secrets? And where was she, anyway?

"Oh, not until this morning. Right before I called...came to find you. Soleil ran into her down by the docks." A gleam in Evian's eye said there was more to the story. "I think it's going to be on the news; they're calling it a solar flare."

"You mean Soleil literally ran into her?"

Evian grinned her answer then elaborated, "They collided over the bay and, between their combined power and Estelle's shocked outburst, took out cellular and Internet service for half an hour over a ten block radius." When she saw Adriel's stricken look, she continued, "Estelle's perfectly fine. She just had to get out of sight until she stopped glowing. I think she got quite a charge out of the experience."

Under normal conditions, undirected angel energy will not affect electronics. Under duress, though, all bets are off. Adriel's first few weeks of being semi-human had cost her former employer more than a few headaches when the energy fouled up the cash register, her car stereo, and her GPS. The cell phone in Adriel's pocket hadn't fared any better, and she still maintained it was this phenomenon and not ineptness in the kitchen that made her produce such lousy coffee.

Leave it to Estelle, though, to collide with the only other supernatural being in a mile-wide area. The corners of Adriel's mouth twitched a little.

"Does that mean you'll help us? If we help you, I mean." Soleil flashed a hint of Bambi eyes while Terra's face gave away nothing of her thoughts. A sudden spark of insight showed Adriel how heavily Soleil's hopes were pinned on mounting a side mission to pull her sister from the darkness at the same time as busting Julius out of Malachiel's prison.

When Adriel felt the sudden ping of conviction that had always preceded an assignment from on high, she stilled to make sure she wasn't just mistaking her own desire to help for an actual directive. The ping came again with an electric pulse, and she knew if more than a minute or two went by without her communicating agreement, the next jolt would be harder. Adriel's erstwhile bosses didn't mess around.

The pause lengthened while she rifled through the catalog of history stored in her head for a time when a guardian angel had ever been assigned to assist a Fae and came up empty. Maybe she shouldn't have been surprised at the offbeat assignment, given her unique position among her kind.

"Yes, I'll help." A sigh escaped while Adriel sent a mental note homeward and received the bare minimum response—another tiny ping. It still hurt to be ignored. *Funny the Powers could hear me just fine when I accepted an assignment, though.* Chances were good the headache she'd been battling was going to make its way to a lower part of her body before this was all over. Was there a pill for that?

She let the three of them have a moment to bask in the triumph of getting her on their side before lowering the boom. "But only if you agree to some stipulations." Masks of wariness fell over their faces. An eternity of political intrigue among the Fae had honed their ability to prevaricate to a fine edge. While bound to speak it, *truth*, to them, is not an absolute, but is measured in degrees of need to know so tiny that a statement of irrefutable fact could have a lie of omission buried at the heart of it. Refusal of an assignment was not an option if Adriel wanted to remain a guardian in good standing, but who was she kidding? That ship was already bounding across the sea—and not on her maiden voyage, either. Becoming earthbound had turned her into an outcast anyway, so if anything these faeries had to say posed more of a problem than she wanted to deal with, the Powers That Be could go scratch.

Nothing would stop Adriel finding and rescuing Julius, but on her own terms, and without being bound to helping a devious faerie who might have chosen darkness.

"Swear an oath that you will answer any question I ask of you to the fullest extent of the truth."

To Evian's frowning surprise, Adriel deadpanned, "Underestimating me already? Your reputation for treacherous speech is well known. It's not my first time dealing with someone from the Fae lands." Direct eye contact belied any humor in the words and Evian stood to swear an oath.

Laying her fingertips on Adriel's wrist, she avowed to be truthful to a fault. The tingle of Fae honesty prickled the skin along the angel's arms and up her spine. Each sister took the turn. By the time Terra begrudgingly promised fealty, Adriel's skin felt like a thousand spiders danced across it.

"First question, Why the sudden effort to save your sister after a hundred years of leaving her to her own choice?"

"Circumstances have changed." Terra snapped out her answer and earned a hard look.

One more terse comment that provided no enlightenment and Adriel would try to angel out a second time and take her chances getting back to the surface. Getting wet wouldn't kill her, and the sooner she was out of here, the sooner she could find a way to free Julius on her own.

Soleil nudged Terra with a sharp elbow. "Vaeta told Julius she had been coerced into helping Malachiel capture him."

"Do you believe that?" Adriel let her eyes rest on Evian since she was the one who had gone to the effort of setting up this meeting in the first place.

"Him? Yes. He faithfully repeated everything she asked him to say." Evian focused on the bowl in the center of the table, repeated the gesture that was currently keeping Adriel dry, and leaned over to blow gently across the mirrored surface.

Amid the ripples rose a hazy image of Julius standing in the shadows of what looked to Adriel like the exterior of an abandoned building. He looked haggard, but whole.

"I have a message for Evian from Vaeta; *tell my sisters I need them.*" He whispered as the moment replayed in the watery scrying mirror. "Her words have the ring of truth, and if not for her I would not have been able to contact anyone in the outside world. Even if you can't help me, you should find a way to free Vaeta from the darkness. Find the earthbound angel. Tell her…" Playback cut off there and began again.

"I have no reason to doubt the conviction of his words to me. Hers to him would be another kettle of carp. She always was the best of us at creative truth-telling."

The phrase was incredibly apt, and if Vaeta had the means to lie well enough to convince Julius of her veracity, the situation was more dangerous than he knew. "Define kettle of carp." If helping him meant helping her, Adriel needed to know what she might be up against.

"Open to different interpretations. Vaeta might have been saying she intended to drag us into the darkness with her." Evian made a flicking motion with her hand, and Julius' voice faded into silence.

"Why don't you just use that," Adriel waved toward the bowl, "to contact her? Doesn't it work both ways?"

"You're familiar with astrology?" It seemed an odd question, but Adriel nodded. "Aquarius—it's an air sign that means water bringer and is also one of Vaeta's names."

Evian's explanation seemed to be missing some parts—like all the parts that actually explained anything, so Adriel pressed her lips shut, leaned back in her chair, and waited to hear more.

"Our two elements have an affinity with each other. Air can carry water, so Vaeta enclosed the moment you've just seen along with the rest of Julius' message in a series of bubbles and sent them here to me. Not the best method of contact and it works only in one direction, but effective for communicating across great distances. By our laws, if she stays away from faerie for a hundred years, she can never return. While our kind doesn't recognize free will to the same depth yours does, we do try to respect the right to choose, and as long as we were convinced it was her choice to stay, we were willing to accept her being lost to us. But, if she was coerced and is in need of rescue, we'll risk all to save her." Evian's words felt like truth.

"If Julius is being held in the dark realm, I'm not sure how much help I will be. For one, I *am* an angel. If I put so much as a toe into the underworld…well, I'm not sure exactly what would happen, but think catastrophic consequences. And for two, in case you haven't noticed, I'm stuck in physical form. Permanently. The only way I can get into the dark realm is to choose to go there when I die."

So I'm still a little bitter, Adriel thought. *Sue me.*

Terra gave the angel a look that said she was beginning to doubt her level of intelligence before pointing out the obvious, "If Julius has not fallen, and neither has he suffered *catastrophic consequences*, clearly he is not trapped in the dark world."

There was a flaw in that logic that had Adriel pinching the bridge of her nose to relieve the pressure in her head. "You're telling me that Julius is trapped in this world while Vaeta remains in the dark world, and the two of them can interact closely enough with each other to blow bubbles." The set looks on all three faces hinted that this was the thing none of them wanted to mention. "The only way that scenario is possible is if the two of them are in a nexus."

A place that only existed in the doorway between worlds.

Evian's resigned nod gave all the confirmation Adriel needed. This mess was getting complicated. The Fringe, an area where two worlds came together, was a place of unpredictability. A nexus was the Fringe on steroids. In order for a portal leading to many worlds to exist, the physical and metaphysical laws of each world must be blended at the meeting point to anchor the door in place. Even the most stable nexus had the potential for chaos.

Adriel sighed. "How much time do we have?"

"Seven days."

"Nothing like leaving things until the last minute." Her attempt to suppress an eye roll failed.

"It's not our fault you took your sweet time getting here." Soleil's hot retort generated another puff of steam.

"I had places to be," Adriel pushed the image of Leith to the back of her mind, though he didn't go willingly, "and no idea I was needed here. Besides, I don't get to choose my assignments." Not anymore. The unspoken comment burned at nerves already raw.

"Now," she leveled a look at the three sisters, "tell me the rest."

"The rest of what?" Identical expressions of feigned innocence failed to impress. Julius had given them a message that they were doing their best not to relay. Adriel would have that information or be done here. She crossed her arms and waited.

"Tell Adriel not to come after me," Estelle spoke from behind Adriel who jumped at the sound of her voice. "Blasted fool. Stubborn in life, foolish in death, and not even being promoted to..." Estelle paused as though searching for the correct word, "...guardian angel in training has improved that particular character trait." The second trainee slash personal guardian appeared much as she had in life. A gently-aged firecracker of a woman.

Wispy curls of hair faded by time from a rich sable to a warm gray framed a round face with dimpled cheeks. Fine lines and creases belied a lifetime of laughter where they edged her eyes and a bow-shaped mouth. Estelle had been a looker back in the day, no mistake. Adriel filed away Estelle's hesitation at using the word angel to describe herself for further reflection.

"You have a bad habit of sneaking up on people." The mild rebuke only brought a fleeting smile to snapping gray eyes before the frown of concern returned.

"Sorry." Maybe so, but being sorry never seemed to stop the sneaking. Evian spirited a fifth chair from somewhere and wedged it in around the already crowded table. "We're going after him anyway, right? What's the plan?"

When Adriel didn't answer right away, Estelle became agitated. "He was helping you, and you're not going to do anything?"

"He doesn't want my help. Isn't that what you just said?" The force of Estelle's disapproval prickled over her mentor's skin while the three faerie sisters remained silent but watchful. Adriel held no illusions that they had more than a polite concern for Julius as long as someone helped them rescue their sister. What she needed most was more information.

As a guardian angel, it had been her job to encourage her charges toward the path of light while still allowing them the freedom of choice, which meant her awareness of the ways the forces of darkness operated was mostly peripheral. Observing a thing is rarely as informational as experiencing it.

Right up until taking on Billy the Earthwalker, her main concern had been to help her charges make better choices while occasionally saving them from their own folly. Out and out battle was never part of the job description. Warrior angels normally handled those types of confrontations, and even they were only called in when circumstances became dire. Adriel had gone well past the limits of her orders to banish the evil Billy from the physical body he had taken over. Accepting mortal help had been an order of magnitude beyond the limits of her authority. Now that she was paying the price for her rash behavior, she was determined not to make the same mistake again. Fool me once, and all that jazz.

"What he wants and what he needs are two different things. We can't just leave him in danger." The level of energy coming off Estelle intensified until it caught in Adriel's throat and made her ears buzz, but she was no mere mortal to be cowed by a show of power. Enjoying that fact that she could once again do so, she lifted a finger to indicate she'd handle this before the faeries got involved.

Adriel reached into that small, silent place inside and radiated a calm that fell like a blanket over the vibrating electricity and cut it off like the flipping of a switch.

"Was I doing it again?" Estelle said.

The internal mentor didn't mind saying she was a little proud of what Estelle could produce, and with such minor effort, too.

"What in our history together makes you think I would allow Julius to remain imprisoned? Get a grip, Estelle."

Chapter 6

Evian led the way back to dry land, flicked away the underwater breathing charm, and handed Adriel a small white shell with a delicate pink pearl interior.

"Hold it to your ear, and you will be able to reach me at any time. Put it in your mouth and you will be able to breathe underwater should you need to return to the grotto without me. I trust you will remember the way."

There was only time to shoot her a raised eyebrow and see the smirk it put on her face before Evian turned and sank below the surface, leaving not so much as a ripple to mark her passing.

Adriel hadn't taken ten steps back toward the heart of the city before the base needs of her human body made themselves known. Between the skirmish with Leith and the time underwater, it felt like a week since she'd eaten or slept. She could crawl in under a bush somewhere and get an hour or two of shuteye once the nagging beast in her belly was soothed, so finding food zoomed straight to the top of the list.

Shoulders hunched, Adriel started to shove the charmed shell into her pocket where she encountered the hard plastic case of her cell phone and the reminder that she still had calls to return.

Her finger hovered over the keypad while she considered her options. There was her former charge, Amethyst, the woman who had essentially dragged Adriel into this whole mess in the first place. Not that Ammie was to blame for the Earthwalker that went after her friends. Or for Adriel's choices when it came to dealing with the situation. Amethyst and the three women who formed her circle had acted selflessly by putting themselves in harm's way to stop a demon.

One, or more likely, all of the four women would drop everything and come to Adriel's rescue if she made the call. Even in the face of danger, they would come because Estelle and Julius were grandparents to one of them, and therefore precious to all—but that wasn't the only reason. They would come for Adriel. Because she mattered enough that they had pulled her into their circle with warmth and acceptance. Not because Adriel had power. Not because she had anything other than herself to offer them. Most definitely not because she had done anything to deserve their allegiance. Just because their hearts were true and open and full of love.

Should she call on them now? There would be questions. Valid questions to which they deserved answers Adriel wasn't ready to give. Still holding the phone, Adriel moved to shove the seashell into her other pocket and found a small wad of paper that delayed her decision.

When her fingers closed over the folded money, she sent up a prayer of thanks. A little over a hundred dollars, her last pay from working at the bakery, but enough to fill her belly and maybe find a cheap room for the night. Now that she had an assignment, chances were good the Powers would leave her here long enough to complete it. A night's sleep would clear her head and give her time to make some plans.

Phone calls could wait for the next day when she could better frame the explanation and had something concrete to tell them. Nothing cowardly about that, right?

46

Resolute, Adriel turned back toward the noise and rush of the city where there were hamburgers, and donuts, and fries, and pizza. A mere block away from the park a flashing neon sign caught her eye and drew it to a board mounted on the wall with the day's specials marked out in chalk. A turkey club sandwich with a side of fries at a price that would not deplete her meager funds unduly sounded like heaven.

Inside, out of the glaring sun, the tiny pub was blessedly cool and dark enough that her eyes needed a moment to adjust. A long bar polished to gleaming spanned the area behind a dozen or so tables. Background music, heavy on guitars and wailing vocals, was low enough to talk over but loud enough to enjoy if you liked that type of thing. Flickering neon advertising beer in red and blue centered a handful of signed celebrity photos, one of whom Adriel recognized as a former charge. Those Hollywood types were always on the verge of selling their souls for the right part. It had taken all her ingenuity to stop him making an irrevocable deal while concealing her true nature. Adriel wondered who was working with him now.

The man behind the bar kept up a running chatter with his patrons while efficiently serving food and drink. His narrow face and dark, beady eyes gave him a ratlike appearance that was only softened somewhat by a wide grin. He greeted Adriel warmly and offered a menu, which she refused in favor of the special from the board.

As hungry as she was, Adriel ordered two sandwiches while ignoring sidelong looks from a stick-sized woman whose neck was almost too thin to hold up her head. She watched each bite with an intensity that bordered on intrusive, her expression horrified. Without thinking about it, Adriel tuned in to the woman's deepest emotions and found that she had become trapped into thinking food was evil. What a sad way to live.

Broken hearted for the woman, but unwilling to cross a line and force the issue, Adriel did the only thing she could do under the circumstances and turned a smile her way. The smile of an angel carries power. Not the kind that alters free will, but offers enough comfort to lift emotional burdens, if only for a moment. It was all Adriel had to give.

So caught up in the plight of the perpetual dieter, Adriel didn't hear the door when it opened behind her or see who entered. What she did see was the smile sliding off the proprietor's face like wax melting off a candle.

"The usual?" He said to the newcomer, who took the seat on Adriel's left. She turned her head just in time to see Leith's nod.

"Hello, Adriel."

"Leith." Why was he here?

"You just seem to be turning up everywhere." The tingle his voice created had nothing at all to do with getting a new assignment, and everything to do with flutters lower in her body. Unlike an assignment, these feelings could be ignored.

"As do you. I don't believe in coincidence." In Adriel's line of work, a genuine coincidence was rarer than hair on a bald man's head. "Are you following me?"

"If I said I felt you here and had to come, would that make me sound pathetic?"

"Depends on why. We didn't exactly hit it off well enough for you to waste time flirting. If the..." she lowered her voice so no one would hear, "package has been delivered. I think our business is done."

"Not even close, Sweetheart. You and me? Trust me. We're only getting started." The smile on his face took the threat from his tone and turned it into a promise. Light eyes met an annoyed gaze and the smile deepened. "The package,"

Adriel heard the air quotes even if he declined to make them, "has definitely not been delivered. Besides, I think we are destined to help one another, and I can't say I dislike the prospect. All I'm asking is for you to give me a chance."

"A chance to what? Show me your third personality?" She scoffed at him. "You remind me of someone I used to know. He had a silver tongue and, as it turns out, a black heart. Full of promises and lies, but always with the best of intentions. As I recall, he ended up paving the road to his new home with them."

"Did you just compare me to the devil?"

"If the horns fit, and if they go with the cape...." Adriel's brain caught up to the conversation. "Wait, what do you mean by not delivered? I saw her heading toward the light."

The look he gave her said plainer than words how extremely clueless he thought she was.

"Given the fact that she followed you in here, I'd say it's a safe bet she didn't cross over." He nodded his head to indicate a spot behind and to the right and Adriel swiveled her head to see nothing but empty space.

"I think you're seeing things." She pulled the cash out of her pocket and laid a twenty on the table, but before she could pull her hand back, Leith covered it with his own and gently squeezed. The contact triggered a vivid mental image of him pulling fire from the air and hurling it toward the rising darkness, but his fire wasn't strong enough, and the roiling black cloud swallowed him whole.

The vision left Adriel shaking with a sense of profound loss.

Could she turn her back on him and leave him to that fate when he had asked outright for her help? This was uncharted territory for her—seeing what might happen and being allowed to choose whether or not to act. What little free will she harbored on her human side clashed with her angel sense of destiny. Nothing like having a split personality to make a girl feel confident.

"What makes you think I need help, anyway?" Or more help than three faeries and a fledgling angel. Not that he needed to know about them just yet.

"Well, you weren't exactly what I'd call a ball of fire in that alley. I mean, if that's your best work, you need somebody. It might as well be me."

Yanking her hand out from under his, she attempted to shrivel him into a raisin with a hot glare. "You know nothing about me or my best work, or even what put me in that alley to begin with." Her voice rose high enough to attract the attention of other customers and so, with an effort, she lowered it back to just above a whisper. "You have no idea."

"Galmadriel. Guardian angel since, well, since forever, I guess. Forced an Earthwalker out of his chosen vessel and the guy lived. You're already well on your way to being a legend. The darkness knows you now."

"You left out the part where I didn't do it alone and one of the women helping me crossed over before her time, so I sent another human over to get her while I used a couple of ghosts to help me anchor the bridge." Bitterness tinged each word. Maybe there had been a better way, but if there had, it was too late now. "We weren't strong enough to hold, and when the bridge went, it dragged me along with it. Now I'm anchored to the physical world, can't depend on what powers are left to me, and am considered so much of a menace that my bosses have cut off most forms of direct contact with me." Legend? Right.

"Okay, so that part isn't common knowledge." He curled his lips under to keep from grinning, and Adriel wanted to smack him. "Doesn't change the outcome, though.

Vanquishing an Earthwalker without killing the host makes you a total badass."

There was that description again. She'd never been able to figure out how that particular part of one's anatomy could determine strength. Something else niggled at her. "Didn't you just say I needed you because I didn't live up to your standards five minutes after regaining consciousness in a strange alley? And now I'm a bad—you know. Stick out your tongue so I can check if it's forked."

Leith's husky laughter slithered over the skin, tantalized and compelled a similar response. This whole situation was absurd.

"I can help. I know things. Things your Powers won't or can't tell you. Maybe you're better than me, maybe not, but if we work together, there's no stopping us. Trust me, Adriel. I'm on your side."

"Trust you? I don't know you, and I'm not even sure what you are." Not straight human—that much was certain. Not a dark thing or he would not have concerned himself with saving a ghost from the darkness. Tuning in, Adriel sensed nothing of the Fae about him. What did that leave? Wizard or warlock, maybe—and yet he didn't smell like one of those, either.

An odd tone came into his voice. "Does it matter as long as I'm trying to help? Maybe I'm just like you—not one thing or another."

"You're like the devil on my shoulder," the retort held no heat.

"You sure I'm not the angel?" His voice purred in my ear seductively. Leith picked up the money, handed it back to her before she had a chance to protest, and paid for both meals. With his hand on Adriel's elbow, they left the pub together.

Based on the electric feel of his hand on her flesh, she'd have laid that twenty on the table to bet he was no angel.

Maybe she wasn't one anymore, either.

***

As the pair stepped out into the fading day, streetlights twinkled on across the city reminding Adriel she should be looking for a place to sleep. Ignoring Leith's presence as best she could, she took a moment to think. The cheaper hotels were going to be on the north side of town, a fifteen-minute walk from here if the map in her head was correct. Before landing herself in this situation, flitting from place to place took no more work than a thought and sleep was only a quaint notion. Those were the abilities she missed the most right this minute. Admittedly, she hadn't tried a spatial jump since getting back a few of her powers. Lacking finesse and fine control over them made results unpredictable at best and disastrous at worst. Plus there was the visibility factor. A woman her size appearing and disappearing into thin air was bound to attract unwanted attention.

"Thank you for the food," she said dismissively and turned her feet northward.

"See you around, Adriel." He drew out the name into long syllables and pronounced it Ahh-dree-elle.

He was gone before she could mutter the entirely unoriginal comeback, "Not if I see you first."

Adriel was still staring after Leith when her phone rang. Out of reflex, she answered. Kathleen Canton, Kat to her friends—among which Adriel was lucky to count herself— didn't even waste time with hello. "218 Canal Street. There's a key hidden under a loose shingle on the back of the garage. Fifth row up, seventh from the left. Pull it out gently and slide it to the right. You can use the place for as long as you need it."

"How did you…"

"Know you would need a place to stay? Please. Remember who you're talking to. It's Ammie and Reid's cottage house. The one they lived in when they got married. Reid kept it for when he has to spend time in the city on foundation business."

"I can't…I don't want to intrude."

An icy silence on the other end lasted several seconds before Kat said evenly, "218 Canal Street. Use the key. Don't make me come down there." The threat was real.

Kat is a powerful psychic and medium, but what does she think she's going to do? Give me a bad Tarot card reading? I'm an angel for crying out loud. That ought to earn me a modicum of respect, Adriel thought.

"I…"

Kat cut the argument off. "There's a service that keeps the place clean, and Reid arranged to have the fridge stocked up. If you need anything, you're to call one of us—which you'll be doing anyway because you know Julie is concerned about Julius. We won't talk about how long you've been ducking our phone calls."

Adriel couldn't help the grin spreading across her face. A more loyal group of women never existed, and given the length and breadth of her experience with history, that's saying something. "You're not worried about repercussions from ordering a higher being to do your bidding?"

"Friend first, angel second. That's how we roll." Kat's grin came across even through the phone. "It's little enough to be able to do. Besides, what are you going to do? Smite us for trying to help?"

"Fine. I'll go. And tell Reid I said thanks."

"Good. Get some sleep. We'll talk tomorrow." With that being both a promise and a threat, a beep signaled the ending of the call.

"Yes, I'm sure we will," Adriel said to no one before heading back the way she had come. Canal Street was fairly close to the park entrance. A coincidence you say. Really? Don't you know who angels work for?

Chapter 7

"Your friends seem nice." The voice in Adriel's ear startled her hard enough to shoot her pulse up to ear-pounding levels. She whirled to see the spirit of the girl from the alley who, as Leith had warned, was far from crossing over.

"You're not...you didn't..."

"Nope, still here." The lilt in her voice sounded downright cheerful. "Sylvie Price." She held out a hand then pulled it back in dismay when she remembered a solid person wouldn't be able to shake it.

"Adriel." Offering no last name because she didn't have one, Adriel said, "You know you are..."

"Dead? Sure. I was there, remember?" Sylvie tossed her head to free caramel-colored eyes from a swing of mousy hair. Her reaction to finding herself suddenly among the existentially challenged defied the norm. Most ghosts upon learning of their demise tend to be considerably less tickled by the prospect.

People were beginning to notice something off about the tall redhead, and why wouldn't they? For all they knew, she was talking to thin air.

"Walk and talk," Adriel commanded and turned toward Canal Street. "What can you tell me about your...about how it happened?" A sideways glance and her face told most of the story. Sylvie's next sentence came as no surprise.

"Well, there was this guy named Dante—except I don't think that was his real name—he was in my ethics class." Her lips twisted as the irony struck home. "He could talk about anything, you know? Like with passion and fire. Well, anyway, he was arguing with the professor about something, and our eyes met. It was like, right out of a movie or something."

The rest of her story played out like an old cliche. Good girl meets bad boy and falls hopelessly in love while bad boy uses her for his own sordid reasons. This story ended with cold death in a dirty alley. Only there was more.

"Dante's in with a bunch of pretty dark people. I think it might be like a cult or something. You know, where people worship the devil." Sylvie's voice dropped to a whisper just as they turned down Canal Street. "They call themselves Knights of the Fulcrum."

The headache that had been coming and going all day finally took up permanent residence between Adriel's eyes and proved it was the kind of noisy neighbor that cranked the stereo up to full blast.

Fulcrum.

The point of balance. Three times in one day the concept of balance had come up. You ask any angel—if you can pin one down—and they'll tell you they don't believe in coincidence. "Tell me everything you remember."

Everything, as it turned out, was almost nothing. Dante had been very careful to keep Sylvie isolated from outside contact. What little she did know had come from shameless eavesdropping and conjecture.

"Do you think he knows I'm…you know, dead?"

"Yes, I'm sure he does." Treacherous truth wouldn't give her the comfort of a harmless white lie, but Adriel had nothing else to offer. There's no Santa Claus and angels mustn't fib.

"Because you think he killed me, right? Well, I know it wasn't him." Despite defending him hotly, Sylvie exhibited doubts. "Dante was in class when it happened, so it must have been someone else."

"Then you didn't see your killer." Adriel made it a statement, not a question because the fear that she might have been betrayed by her lover put a quaver in Sylvie's voice whenever she mentioned his name.

"I heard someone call out to me, and then I saw the carvings on the knife." The tiny hairs on the back of Adriel's neck tickled to standing. There was something here."

"Tell me everything you remember about the knife."

"It had a black handle and a design carved into the blade." Sylvie traced a triangular shape in the air. "Dante didn't hurt me and you're going to help me prove it." Clearly, the spirit had no idea to whom she was issuing orders. "I mean it. You help me or I'll..."

A raised eyebrow and steely gaze demand an end to that sentence. What threat could the ghost possibly use on an earthbound angel?

"...I'll follow you everywhere you go." When Adriel shrugged off her threat, Sylvie upped the ante. "I'll talk. Talk. Talk. Talk. Talk. Talk. Until it drives you crazy. Day and night. Night and day. Talk. Talk. Talk. You won't have a minute's rest until you agree to help me."

Poor Sylvie needn't have bothered resorting to coercion. Both parties interests were aligned, and it was Adriel's job to help her anyway.

"Imaginative threat. I like your style."

Sylvie opened her mouth to make good on her plan, and Adriel gestured for her to stop. "Save the chatter. I'll help. After…" A sharp word interrupted an excited squeal, "I get some sleep. Come back in the morning."

Fading out like the Cheshire cat, Sylvie took herself off to wherever it is errant spirits go when they're not bugging those few people who can hear or see them.

Walking down the second block of Canal Street, Adriel knew she was in the right place. With crisply painted lavender siding and eggplant colored shutters, it practically screamed Amethyst. The only thing more pointed would have been a purple neon beacon flashing the woman's name. Gustavia had had a hand in the landscaping unless Adriel missed her guess.

Petunias, a shade darker than bubblegum pink, cascaded from planter boxes along the porch railing to trail blossoms behind a bank of fragrant wild roses right at the end of their blooming cycle. Not much more than three feet of mowed grass separated the sidewalk from the rose bushes, and a pair of potted geraniums flanked the paved entrance.

Running along the right side of the house, the narrow driveway terminated at a single bay garage painted the same deep purple as the shutters. Feeling a little like a trespasser, Adriel quickly located the key right where Kat had said it would be and let herself into the house. The aftermath of an adrenaline-fueled day had left her shaking with exhaustion, so she hit the bathroom and the bed in that order.

Chapter 8

Intending to be out of bed at sunrise, Adriel let soft sheets, fluffy pillows, and a mattress with just the right amount of firmness seduced her into dispensing with every single good intention. When her feet finally hit the floor, it was past eight o'clock in the morning, and the only thought in her head had to do with scouring the kitchen for something dark, hot, and full of caffeine.

Dressed in a borrowed tee that could only have belonged to Reid because one of Amethyst's would have felt scandalously short, she padded into the galley kitchen and confronted the beast that common sense told her would provide, rich, dark nectar if only she could figure out how to tame it. All gleaming stainless steel, it hunkered on the counter and eyed Adriel with distrust as if it knew she was out of her depth.

The handles and jets and a tiny glass pot looked nothing like the simple machines she had barely mastered. This was the dragon of coffeemakers. The king of the dragons, really, and, as a mere mortal, Adriel was outclassed before she even figured out where to put the water.

In the third drawer she opened, she found the instruction manual. All forty-six pages of it. Nothing meant to pass water through ground coffee should be that complicated. Adriel was about to give it up as a bad job when a laminated card with a quick start guide fell out from between the pages. She followed the instructions to the letter and produced the second worst cup of coffee in recent history—which she then doctored up with a ridiculous amount of cream and sugar, and drank down in three huge gulps anyway. The coffee was strong enough to strip paint off a wall, but at least she was finally fully awake enough to take in her surroundings.

Half again the size of her last digs, the house still qualified as tiny. On one side of the open floor plan living space, the compact kitchen featured a two-seater breakfast bar on the left that doubled as counter space, and to the right sat a small table. Behind them was a centered sink with a small section of countertop on either side. The range occupied one corner and the refrigerator the other.

The whole thing looked out onto a comfortable living room with a cathedral ceiling. A sectional sofa covered in plush tan fabric and dotted with brightly patterned throw pillows—in shades of purple naturally—dominated the small space, providing a generous amount of seating given the room's narrow dimensions.

Toast and eggs soaked up the rest of the swill that couldn't remotely be called coffee before it could chew through Adriel's stomach lining. She bet people with brewing skills as bad as hers were the reason coffee shops were invented. To save them from an untimely, acid stomach-related death.

Half an hour later, the kitchen was tidy, the bed made, and she was just stepping out of the shower when she realized I had nothing clean to wear. Borrowing something to sleep in was one thing, but Reid's dresser drawers were not hers to rummage through with abandon. Not that he would protest—Adriel knew, without a doubt, she was welcome to borrow whatever she might need, but his waist was inches larger than hers, and she preferred not to go with the cinch, pleat, and belt routine to hold up a pair of pants.

As she picked up her phone from the table where she had stashed it the night before, a thought occurred. If she could retain the cell phone by virtue of it being on her person when the powers bounced her from one place to the next, why not carry a few more things? A couple changes of clothes, some non-perishable food items, toiletries, and a small first aid kit would fit into a small backpack for a start.

Once upon a time, Adriel had been the guardian angel of a Boy Scout leader who preached endlessly about always being prepared. Now she was ready to admit he might have been on to something.

Dressed temporarily in the best fitting items she could cadge from the closet, she consulted her mental map for the closest thrift store and set off at a brisk walk. The more she thought about it, the more she liked the idea. She could be one of those vagabonds who whisk off from place to place at a moment's notice. Okay, so she was lucky if she got that much warning, and she was the whiskee, never the whisker, but you get the idea. A few necessities that she could count on having with her at all times might lessen the impact of waking up in weird places alone.

"That's an LL Bean backpack," said the friendly cashier at the thrift store. "You know those have a lifetime warranty, right? It's in great condition now, but when it wears out, you can exchange it for a new one."

Lifetime warranty. Interesting concept. Whose lifetime? The buyer or the company manufacturing the item? Thinking too much about the finality of death was not going to be super useful to at the moment, given the gravitas of my current situation. Adriel had no idea what her lifespan might be. The same as any other human? Longer? Or, if she tangled with too many demons, a whole lot shorter.

Eventually, she realized the cashier was looking at her with naked curiosity, so she paid for her purchases and skedaddled out of there before finding out how many more items of clothing had the potential to outlive their owners. What a depressing thought.

Adriel's next stop took her into a corner drug store where she added travel-sized toiletries and a basic first aid kit to the pack. With each addition, the rucksack became heavier while her heart lightened. These things were inconsequential in the grand scheme of things, but they were hers. There was satisfaction to be had when she settled their weight between her shoulder blades and tugged the straps into a comfortable position. Being proactive felt amazing.

"I had a backpack just like that, only it was pink instead of blue. And it wasn't an LL Bean, it was from Walmart. The straps were wider." Sylvie was either following through on her plan to talk Adriel into submission or her mouth was in its natural mode. On.

"So, really, nothing like this one, then." Adriel muttered while trying to keep from moving her lips too much and drawing attention from passersby.

Chapter 9

The beep of an incoming text signal interrupted the next spate of Sylvie's nattering, and the display showed Kat's number.

Go to 157 East Hammond Street. Knock on the door three times and ask for Cassandra. She has connections to the spirit world and a story to tell you.

Before there was time to text any of the half dozen questions that popped into Adriel's head, the tone sounded a second time.

Just go.

Bossy.

I have my own connections to the spirit world—she texted back and received a frowning emoticon in reply.

Okay, I'm going.

Kat's timing created a tricky situation. Taking Sylvie along to visit Cassandra seemed like a bad idea, and telling her to buzz off sounded like a worse one. Only one solution came to mind.

"Sylvie, do you remember the man who tried to help you yesterday?"

"The blond with the piercing stare? Sure."

"Could you," a short battle waged in Adriel's head and she barely managed not to say the phrase *latch on*, "find him the same way you found me?"

"Easy, why?"

"He got there ahead of me. Maybe he saw something helpful. You should go," *talk him half to death*, "ask him."

Brightened by the thought of doing something proactive, Sylvie sped off to look for Leith.

The section of town where Cassandra live had its roots in the manufacturing boom during the late 1920s. A row of six houses, identical save for color and trim options, had been built for the department heads of the hulk of a baked bean factory that was crumbling into ruin at the dead end of the street. Some were grateful to see an end to the smell of cooking beans, while others in the neighborhood cursed the technological advancements that had finally taken the factory into a smaller building and cost many jobs in the process.

By the end of the century, automation had displaced most of the workforce, including the supervisors, and the homes were now privately owned. Number 157 was the shabbiest of the six, and badly in need of a little TLC. Peeling paint littered the porch floor where it met the wall, and tattered plastic sheeting stood in place of glass in the smaller of the two windows. Creaking sounds underfoot boded ill for anyone dumb enough to jump up and down on the porch, and Adriel walked as gingerly across the sagging floorboards as she could.

Each knock echoed loudly on the weathered, but surprisingly sturdy front door, and minutes passed before there were sounds of someone moving around on the other side.

"Who's there?" A high-pitched voice came through the door at about the height of a pre-teen child.

"My name is Adriel. Can I speak to Cassandra? Kat sent me." Hopefully, Cassandra wasn't expecting a secret handshake. This all seemed dramatically clandestine.

"Kat? Don't know nobody named Kat."

What was that other name she used? Madame something, related to weather. Not storm. Breeze? No. Something else.

"Madame Zephyr sent me." That was it.

"Well, why didn't you say that to begin with?" The door creaked on aged hinges as it swung wide, and Adriel followed the four-foot nothing form into the dark recesses. The place looked like something whipped up by a Hollywood set designer as the perfect model of a haunted house. Wallpaper yellowed with age and browned by water stains was loosening its hold on the walls in perfectly artistic shreds. Scarred woodwork, flickering bulbs that gave off flaccid light, and carpets worn threadbare gave way into a kitchen that was cheerful by contrast.

A vintage, porcelain-coated, cast iron range rested in the heart of the room. Aqua and white, its lines reminded me of a classic car. Built for speed and cocky with it, the versatile range top featured a set of gas burners on one side and wood on the other. A tank for heating water hung on the side of the wood burning box and a pair of warming ovens with rounded doors spanned the top. It was a thing of beauty compared to the modern, box-like options currently in vogue.

Sunny yellow walls contrasted nicely with the blue-green porcelain and made the room that much brighter. Worn to a flat white in the middle, the textured linoleum carried a floral pattern in the lower traffic areas. Painted aluminum cabinets lined one wall and windows lined the other.

When Cassandra turned to offer a seat at the table, Adriel realized the figure she had mistaken for a child was merely a woman made child-sized by advanced age. Compared to the stooped form, Adriel felt like a giant.

"You're the angel." Shrewd eyes roved speculatively from a face tilted sideways, tracing the shape of unseen wings.

"I am. Kat says you have a story to tell me."

Cassandra ignored the invitation to tell what she knew. Instead, she blinked twice and a chill stole across Adriel's skin as she heard the popping sounds of the seer's spine straightening. The age fell from her like shattered glass to break upon the floor and revealed the woman as she must have looked when she was new. Bright and shining with the kind of beauty that ran rampant in the home Adriel could no longer reach. Cassandra's was a soul that had chosen to make many trips to the physical world—this being her last. Hard-earned wisdom afforded the human woman a small measure of the very same grace Adriel had once commanded with ease, but which now sat on her with much less comfort.

A small hand lifted to rest against Adriel's cheek, while eyes lit by white fire burned deep and revealed Cassandra for what she was. An oracle.

"Seek not your grace in the faces of others, in the wheels of time, nor mourn for its passing and home. Tis not gone, nor does it lie in subdued slumber. Tis not diminished by circumstance or flesh. Embrace your path, and that which blinds you to your own light will fall away. All that you have ever been, or will ever be lies within you now as it always has." Power laced Cassandra's voice with a quality that made each word fall with the ringing sound of a hammer on a bell.

A few seconds passed and the onus upon the oracle drifted away, taking that sense of youth along with it to leave her body bent and twisted once again, the strange light gone.

"Every psychic in a hundred mile radius felt it when you dropped out of the sky. You're the answer to our prayers. It's

66

getting bad out there, and I was beginning to think this was the start of the end times. Then you came streaking down out of the blue, and we knew you had come to save us all." Her quavering voice picked up the conversation as though nothing had happened. "You'll have a cup of tea and sit a spell." An order, not an invitation. Angel Adriel would have turned on the juice and gotten an answer out of her without the need for niceties. Human Adriel was beginning to wonder if angel Adriel hadn't been somewhat of a jerk when it came to interspecies relationships.

Both aspects of Adriel planted their butts in the seat, and she chose an oatmeal cookie with genuine appreciation. Crisp on the outside, chewy in the middle, just a hint of nutmeg. Perfection.

"What can you tell me about your mission?" Cassandra poured pale tea that smelled faintly of roses into a delicate cup--the best of her meager collection chosen only for special uses, and angel Adriel took another hit in the jerk department.

Picking a path through the conversation to give Cassandra enough information to satisfy, but leaving out the faeries entirely, Adriel described her encounter with Leith and the dead girl from the alley.

Sparse eyebrows enhanced with a shaky line of pencil two shades too dark arched high.

"He took you to his lair?"

"I suppose so." Who uses the word lair outside of a comic book? The word evoked visions of tiptoeing into the Batcave, and brought on a barely held back snort.

"Fancy that."

"You know Leith." Biting down on the questions that threatened to fly out of her mouth, Adriel feigned disinterest. With a tiny smirk playing across her lips and the twinkle in her eye, Cassandra saw right through that ploy.

67

"Hard to avoid him if you're part of the community." By which she must have meant the supernatural community since it was hard to picture him taking an active part in any civic-minded one. "He gets around." What was Adriel supposed to make of that?

She would not ask.

"What do you mean?" Mouth and mind, clearly not in contact with each other.

Another twinkle. "Not romantically, dear. He just seems to have a knack for knowing when his unique abilities are needed."

"He's a vigilante."

Wrong word. Cassandra frowned. "A protector of innocence, more like. Evil things are happening every day. Senseless violence is on the rise. People are so angry, so lost, and hurting each other over the most insignificant things. Murder. Suicide. Families killing their own. It's not normal."

Clouds of despair shadowed her eyes.

"What's more, the dark-spawned have been taking the souls of innocents right out from under your noses, and you angels don't seem to care that it's happening." Gentle accusation tinged the words.

"Don't care? Of course, I care," Adriel insisted, but couldn't hide her shock.

"Ah, I see. You had no idea."

"How long has this been going on?" Biting her lip, Adriel wondered if guardians had been left intentionally out of the loop, or if it was just her. Something like this should have been big news.

Cassandra paused to think. "The first time I heard of it was almost two years ago. A mother who had lost her little boy to cancer asked me to contact him. She was convinced she had seen a shadow lurking around him as he passed, and became frantic to know if he had made it into the light." A shudder ran through her hunched frame. "Rules being what they are, he couldn't tell me everything that happened, but he did tell quite a story about how the bright light flared like fireworks. What he described sounded like an angel battling the darkness to clear his path. After that, I began to hear similar stories from my friends in the local community."

"Just the local community. How widespread is your network?"

"This *is* the information age, my dear. Email, texts. It's easy to spread out and go global."

"Or to sit on pertinent data."

"She wasn't hiding it from you." As if reading Adriel's thoughts, Cassandra reassured.

"Then Kat had no idea this was happening?"

"None. Until we spoke last night, she was as in the dark as you were, which is significant given what happened when you took on that Earthwalker."

"How many people know about that?" Adriel felt like she had just noticed her underwear had been on the outside all day and no one had told her. Information age, indeed.

"Not too many." Cassandra grinned. "Just those of us who were in the psychic blast radius. Twenty or so with enough juice to sense the magnitude of what happened. Our guides put out the word that one of their own needed protection, and to keep quiet about what we had seen, so no one's talking about it."

"That you know of." Adriel repeated hopelessly as a new thought occurred. "And all of them know about me being..." she gestured to her body, "...earthbound?"

A kindly but steady gaze was the only answer. Great. Which was worse? Finding out that the psychic community was larger than she thought, or that it was more connected. Or that people and angels had been talking about her. Adriel's face flushed red hot and her pulse raced.

Cassandras child-sized hand rested on Adriel's briefly. "Nothing, not even death is final, Galmadriel. This is but a turn of the wheel, a moment in time." It was basically the same as her oracle message.

Comforting words, given their simplicity and truth. This too shall pass.

"Thank you, Cassandra. Blessings upon you." Something of Adriel's power flowed between them with a sigh like the breath of a gentle wind, and brought tears to her eyes.

"The honor is mine, Lightworker."

The two women shared a moment of silence before Cassandra spoke again, "You helped save my friend from being taken into the dark."

"Sylvie?"

"Yes, the girl in the alley."

Adriel felt her lips twist, "According to Leith, all I did was get in the way and mes up his plans for saving her."

"Shall we say it was a concerted effort? Sylvie was one of mine. An apprentice like." Sadness put a frown on Cassandra's face. "She had great promise but was easily swayed by pretty words from a treacherous boy with ties to the worst elements in this town. My spirit guides..." her head tilted to the side as she whispered two names, "...do you know them?"

"Different division." An easy explanation for a complicated system. "With limited contact." More like none, given she had been cut off completely from her own people.

"My spirit guides want me to tell you to find out who killed Sylvie. More, they want you to know her death is related to your current assignment." For the first time since Adriel had walked through the door, Cassandra seemed troubled, "Something keeps blocking them from giving me more information. I wonder if that is for your protection or mine. The danger is real, and you will not face it alone." The oracle shone through briefly. "One of your party will fall. Now, take this," she handed Adriel a small cross suspended on a chain. The cheap metal had already shed most of its thin gold plating. "It belonged to Sylvie. Finding her killer is the first step—everything hangs in the balance. Tell her to stop in and say goodbye before she moves on."

"I will do my best, and hope that it will be enough." Cassandra's shoulders sagged with relief.

"Bless you, Lightworker."

"Bless you, old mother." The term was a benediction—one Adriel followed by gently laying her hands on the older woman's head and letting pure healing light flow from them. There is no cure save the final one for old age, but tonight Cassandra would sleep without pain or fear. It was little enough to give her.

Head bowed, she remained in her chair while Adriel let herself out.

Chapter 10

So many thoughts whirled around in Adriel's head, she lost the next hour in aimless wandering and attempting to tame them. It was like trying to do a jigsaw puzzle with half the edge pieces missing. There was no true starting place, and the picture looked like a hot mess.

None of the clues added up to anything that made sense. She wasn't buying the theory there was someone in the underworld foolish enough to try to infiltrate the realm of light. At least not for the sake of bringing about the end of everything. And even if there was some crazy reason, Adriel could not see where she fit into the picture at all.

The only thing she could do was keep her promise to Cassandra and look for Sylvie's killer. Adriel decided to go back to the beginning and see if she could find anything that might link Sylvie's death with this Dante character.

A great plan, but with one drawback. Adriel had no idea where to look for the scene of the crime. Landing in the alley while dead unconscious, and being transported out of there before she had a chance to orient herself had left her with no frame of reference to work from. Sylvie hadn't exactly been a fount of useful information, either. Not that Adriel had thought to ask.

Leith would know. If she had the first clue where to find him, or the inclination to subject herself to what he considered witty banter, which left her with a couple of lousy options. She could methodically search the city like a lunatic on a quest for some fabled artifact, or she could return to the general area of the second alley and...well...use it as ground zero for searching the city like a lunatic on a quest for some fabled artifact. Okay, so there was really only one option with different starting points.

"Adriel!" Caught up in deciding what her next step should be, she failed to notice her proximity to the park where Pam Allen sold pastries out of a food truck most days. "Adriel. It is you."

What do you do when your gut screams at you to run away from a situation bound to turn awkward?

During Adriel's last mission—her first as an earthbound angel—she had fallen pretty much out of the sky and into Pam's life. Maybe fallen is the wrong word, Adriel had been sent to find the man who had killed Pam's brother in a cold-case hit and run accident, reunited the baker with the boy's ghost, and eventually helped his shade to cross over after thirty years. That kind of shared experience creates a strong bond.

Angels are not supposed to bond with the people they help.

After literally landing in Pam's life and turning it upside down, Adriel had done what she was used to doing and left again without so much as a goodbye.

That was how it would have looked to Pam, anyway.

She'd have no idea that the leaving hadn't been under Adriel's control which gave her no choice in the matter. Not the nicest way to treat someone who had been kind enough to provide a job and a place to live. All of which had been repaid by being deserted without explanation.

An apology was the least of Adriel's debts. Hot shame stained her skin as she turned to face the woman she considered a friend and beg forgiveness.

Pam hit Adriel like a freight train before she could get the first word out and hugged her so hard her ribs creaked under the pressure. When she finally pulled back to let Adriel get a good look at her, shock plastered itself all over the angel's face. Pam looked at least ten years younger now that she had gotten closure from the tragedy. Gone were the shadows that once clouded green eyes. Gone were the lines of sadness that had been etched into her face. Pam was a new woman.

She hugged Adriel again, then held her at arm's length. "I'm so happy to see you even if it's going to cost me ten bucks." Pam grinned at the confused frown her words elicited. "Kat bet me that I'd see you again. I thought it was just her way of cheering me up, but I should have known better."

"The woman never gets it wrong."

An awkward silence fell after that until Adriel felt compelled to blurt out, "You must hate me. I'm so sorry. I was on my way to say goodbye when..." She waved a hand to indicate that I'd ended up here. Pam knew better than anyone just how abruptly the Powers could alter time and location.

"I don't hate you. Of course, I don't. As much as I loved having you in my life, I'm not so selfish that I would keep you from doing for others what you did for me. My life is so different now. There are no words to describe how grateful I am." While she talked, Pam linked arms, and half dragged Adriel over to sit at one of the tables that dotted the manicured grass near her truck.

"Stop fretting. All is forgiven. Now tell me what's been happening with you."

"Oh, you know, the same old, same old. Chasing ghosts, finding Julius, learning how to be whatever it is that I am."

74

Aiming for flippant, Adriel missed the mark and hit somewhere between pathetic and bizarre.

Pam regarded her silently for several seconds, then she said, "Something is different."

"Different good or different bad?"

"I'm not sure." She rested her elbow on the table and continued her speculative regard until Adriel started to squirm in her seat. "Want coffee?" The change of subject came out of nowhere.

Pam's coffee? "Uh, yeah." Who wouldn't? The woman worked magic with the roasted bean.

"You won't leave while I get some?"

Adriel shook her head, "No, I'll stay."

From where she sat, she witnessed Pam's short but animated conversation with Hamlin, who carefully avoided looking toward the picnic table while he poured the dark brew. It seemed not everyone had forgiven Adriel for her abrupt departure. His little crush on her probably had as much to do with the animosity as the protectiveness he felt for his business partner. Grudgingly, he handed Pam the cardboard carry tray with two cups and two plates.

When she returned with coffee *and* pie, Adriel wanted to kiss her. If it had any feet, her sweet tooth would have jumped for joy. Hamlin made exceptional graham cracker pie, a northeastern specialty. Perfectly cooked meringue, creamy vanilla filling, and a crumb crust made each bite nothing short of nirvana.

"You've changed." Pam took up the conversation right where she left off and squinted at Adriel shrewdly. "Loosened up a little," she offered only that clarification before asking, "How long have you been here?" A subtle way of asking if I had been dodging her calls.

75

"Not quite a day. I lost a couple of weeks in the transition."

Relief loosened the tightness across Pam's shoulders and around her mouth. "Where are you staying?" Adriel skated past one conversational minefield unscathed, only to land right in the middle of a bigger one.

"Amethyst and Reid have a small house that they don't use much." The admission allowed for having spoken to at least one of the others, but not calling Pam and so, despite wanting to protect her friend, Adriel spilled everything that had happened since waking up in the alley—including that she needed to find her way back there again.

"I can help with that."

"How?" Did Pam have a sixth sense she never talked about? Her answer burst my bubble with a grin.

"The Internet. Crime rates are increasing here, but not so swiftly that a murder wouldn't have made the news. Wait here." Pam retrieved her phone from the truck and spoke briefly with Hamlin again. The result of that conversation netted Adriel a tentative smile and a wave hello, both of which she returned.

Settling back in her seat, Pam accessed the information quickly from one of the local television sites and gave Adriel an address only a block away from where she had landed the second time. "Sylvie Price, aged twenty. Such a shame. Police have taken her boyfriend in for questioning, but he is not considered a suspect at this time. They're asking for anyone with information about the crime to come forward, and then it's the usual statement that the investigation is active and ongoing. I'd bet they won't release the scene for another day or so."

Not happy news since a closed crime scene meant Adriel would have to use a different approach.

"I can't wait that long. I'm going to…"

"Call Kat." They both said at once. Pam giggled—a lighthearted sound given the gravity of Sylvie's demise. With Sylvie unable to identify her killer, Kat might still be able to pick up on something helpful.

"How's Callum?" Adriel changed the subject since this was as involved as she wanted Pam to be in whatever Sylvie had gotten mixed up in. "Did he finally work up the courage to ask you out?"

"Yes." All the humor fell away, and Adriel wondered how long it would take her to spit out the foot she'd just lodged in her own mouth. Pam clammed up tighter than…well…a clam, what else?

"It didn't go well?"

"It went very well."

"Then what? He didn't call?"

"He called."

"Then why does your face look more pinched than a schoolmarm's shoes?"

The comparison earned her a raised eyebrow, and the barest hint of a smile before the mask dropped back over Pam's features.

"It didn't work out. That's all."

"Flipping lie is what that is. Tell me what happened or I'll…" no end to that sentence came readily to mind. What was Adriel going to do? Beat the answer out of her? Not angelic behavior. Unless the butt kicking is of the holy kind and a necessity, she was a pacifist by nature, if not by choice.

Pam bit her lip, and Adriel flashed her best authoritative stare, the one she used on former charges when they needed a poke or a prod delivered from what they assumed was a stranger. Quite effective most of the time.

"He had a thing for *you* and how am *I* supposed to compete with that?" One hand lifted to gesture in Adriel's general direction. "Even in secondhand clothes that fit you poorly, you're the total package. Tall, built, and gorgeous. Porcelain skin, red hair, eyes that see into the soul. Next to you, I feel like a troll."

Adriel wasn't having any of it. "Callum wanted me for no other reason than to stroke his ego." She ignored Pam's snort over her choice of phrase. "In his eyes, I was a pale second to the woman he had admired from a distance for years and a safe bet for keeping his heart intact. Do you want the man?"

"Yes." A whisper that was close to a sigh.

"Then stop acting the fool, and go out with him the next time he asks."

"What if he doesn't?"

"Then you will have to suck it up and ask him out yourself."

"See, that's what I mean. You would never have said *suck it up* before. I think you're embracing peoplehood. Any chance you'll ever embrace anything else?" The waggling eyebrows gave Adriel a hint that Pam was talking romance and that was a hole she had no intention of chasing the rabbit down. Promising to keep in touch, she beat a hasty retreat before Pam started trying to pair her off with Hamlin or something.

Chapter 11

"Do you think this is going to work?" Adriel asked Kat as they ducked under the yellow tape stretched across the mouth of the alley where Sylvie had died.

"Depends." Kat focused most of her attention on the tiny cross dangling from her hand. "Sylvie says she didn't see her killer. Your vision of the attack bears out her story, which leaves me with a needle and haystack situation. I can use the necklace to home in on the psychic residue, but without a lot of luck, we're looking at a long shot. Unless..."

"Unless what?"

"Unless maybe you give it a little shot of miracle juice? Not a lot, just a nudge in the right direction. Or would that be breaking the rules? There are rules, I assume." Kat's nervous chatter filled the silence. "You guys are so hush-hush with that kind of thing." She got a look at the stunned expression on Adriel's face. "No? All right then, I'll just get on with it." The hand holding the necklace twitched twice to set the cross swinging. "I'm not going to get into trouble with your Powers for using a sacred symbol as a pendulum, am I?"

Trying to keep up with Kat when her mind was still stuck on the miracle suggestion, put Adriel a step behind. These things don't just happen at the whim of an angel. There's paperwork to fill out and a ton of red tape. Bureaucracy is inescapable. Even a green-stamped miracle has a waiting period, which is precisely why some people think prayers go unheard.

"Adriel." Kat snapped her fingers for attention. "The longer we hang around here, the more likely we are to get caught. This was your idea, but if you don't think we should do it, you need to tell me now."

"Sorry, I'm distracted. Do it. Hurry."

Kat swung the makeshift pendulum again. Instead of following a smooth arc, the cross vibrated on the end of the chain, bounced, and flashed in erratic circles while she frowned down at it. "That's new and different. Something is interfering with the results."

Or someone. Adriel already had a suspect in mind.

A sudden movement at the mouth of the alley drew their attention to a man making his way toward them. With the sun behind him, it was impossible to see his face.

"You there, this is an official crime scene. You're breaking the law."

Sidling up to him suggestively, Kat purred, "Hey, handsome, is there any way you could overlook it just this once? I'll make it worth your while, big boy."

"Bribing an officer of the law is a felony offense, Ma'am."

"I'll do anything you want."

"Anything? I guess you'll be watching Demolition Man with me this weekend, then." Zack Roman bent to kiss Kat on the nose.

"Really? I offer you anything, and that's what you choose? You could have asked for sexual favors, and all you can think of is making me watch some cheesy movie." Kat kissed him back.

"It's a classic."

Adriel greeted Zack then settled in to listen to them. They squabbled like an old married couple, and it was a joy to hear.

"How did you know where to find me," Kat wasn't the only one with psychic gifts, even if Zack kept common knowledge of his under wraps.

"Please. I *am* a cop; give me some credit for my powers of deduction. Adriel called. That's enough of a rarity that there had to be more to it than girl talk. Then you make some flimsy excuse to take a drive into the city. It wasn't hard to figure out that you would both be drawn to the scene of a murder if you thought there was something you could do to help. Didn't take a psychic to follow that trail."

"My turn," Kat said. "This isn't your case, and you weren't concerned I might be arrested, so you followed me here for a different reason." Her brow furrowed, "You came here to take me out to lunch." She linked an arm in his. "Gregorio's?"

Zack grinned down at her for a second before turning serious again, "That, but I also wanted to talk to Adriel." His face shuttered. "I can't believe I have to ask this, but is there an actual reaper who helps souls cross over?"

"A reaper? Like with a black robe and a scythe?" The question was so far out of left field, she needed clarification.

"Not exactly. They say he wears a red cape."

Leith.

"Oh, him. He's no reaper." Disgust colored her tone, and she followed with a sigh. "What have you heard about him?"

"There have been reports of a man in a cape showing up after someone dies and—this sounds ridiculous—standing guard over the body." When Adriel didn't seem shocked or skeptical, Zack continued, "He's been spotted at two accident scenes, and once near a heart attack victim in a restaurant."

"Is he wanted in connection with any crimes or considered dangerous?"

"Not exactly. None of the deaths were suspicious, but the department is beginning to wonder how he manages to get to the scene ahead of first responders. Is he one of yours? An angel of death?"

It would have been simpler if he was.

"His name is Leith, and he's not a reaper or an angel. Far from it. Actually, I'm not sure exactly what he is other than that he is a practitioner."

"What does that mean?" Kat asked.

"He has certain abilities. Powers. I guess you would call him a wizard."

Zack snorted. "So he's Harry Potter? Is that why he wears a cape?"

A tingle speared across Adriel's sense. The kind she felt whenever Leith was near, so she raised her voice so he could hear, "No, that's just a bad fashion choice."

Kat asked the ultimate question, "Does he work for good or evil?"

"That remains to be seen. From what I can tell, he is trying to help in his own misguided way."

Satisfied for the moment, Zack guided Kat out of the alley after cautioning me not to get caught by one of his brothers in blue. "I'd hate to see you get thrown in jail on obstruction charges."

"You know you'd bail me out," Adriel teased. Kat handed her back the necklace with orders to call if she needed more help.

"You can come out now," Adriel said once they were gone. "I know you're here."

"Why? So you can malign my fashion choices again? That was a low blow." Leith's voice came from somewhere to her left.

"We need to talk. Truce?" When Leith appeared minus the cape, she concealed a smirk. Instead of a Musketeer in search of a brotherhood, he looked like a handsome prince.

"T-truce," she stammered.

Detente lasted about fifteen seconds before he snaked out a hand to grab Sylvie's necklace. Adriel was not having any of it and pulled back. A short but furious tug of war ended with their eyes locked and their hands meeting like those cartoon dogs over the spaghetti. If her breathing had quickened, it was only because of the chemistry between them and not from physical exertion. Even in her most sarcastic thoughts, the cannot-tell-a-lie angel filter reversed her words into truth.

"Adriel." The slow, sweet timbre of his voice went to her head like fine wine. "Adriel." Sharper this time, he demanded her full attention. "Look. It's working."

"It's what? Oh." The necklace tugged hard enough to whip a red mark into her palm. Surprise loosened Adriel's grip to leave Leith holding the thin metal chain by himself. The shock in her eyes mirrored his when the cross went from animated movement to dead still the second her touch fell away.

"See, you need me." A cloud chose that precise moment to block out the sun and cast enough of a shadow over his face that Adriel found it impossible to tell if he was joking or serious. "Together." Trying to maintain a sense of personal distance while holding on to the same slender chain worked about as well as you would expect. Her arm tingled and buzzed at the contact during the entire time they followed the tug of the cross toward the back of the alley. It pulled them into the shadows directly across from the ledge where Adriel landed when she awakened from my trip here, and all the blood drained from her face when she saw the small pile of black feathers that had drifted into the corner.

She picked one up to turn it over and over in her hand. No bit of bird plumage, this. The center line that ran the length of the rachis was made of living silver—tarnished now to a sooty black that matched the soft barbs.

Malachiel.

Had he stood in that very spot while she lay insensible not ten feet away? Picturing him standing just that close and watching her was enough to raise goosebumps over most of Adriel's body. Leith felt the shudder and shake, and gently pulled the feather from her hand.

"Give it to me if it affects you like that." He said it without a trace of mocking—for that, she was grateful. "Besides, I have an idea." Leith gently tugged the necklace from her hand and wrapped the chain tightly around the dusky quill. The swift and sure motions captivated Adriel's attention.

"Take hold of it again," he directed with a surprising amount of compassion. At every turn, the man managed to surprise. She did as he asked and felt the chain jerk back to life. They didn't have far to go; a handful of yards toward the mouth of the alley, the tugging cross indicated an expanse of brick wall covered in graffiti.

Like two powerful magnets drawn to each other, the cross slapped against the wall with an audible ping and landed on a tag—the individual signature of the artist. This tag consisted of nine overlapping circles positioned around the letter D. As symbolism goes, this was on the simple side. Sylvie's Dante must have taken his name from the historical figure who wrote convincingly of the nine circles of hell. Adriel learned she could say hell when she meant the actual place.

Compelled to do it by some unknown force, she brushed a hand over the tag. Whatever working had been done there, the magic rose to taste her touch; dark power shimmered off the wall in greasy waves. "You feel it, don't you?" Leith whispered.

In answer, she gave him an enigmatic look then, closed her eyes and channeled what bits of grace she could pull to the surface and sent it all toward the wall. Light sparked and sizzled into the nooks and crannies of brick baked to a dark pink by time and sun. A pattern formed and with one look, Adriel went nauseous and weak. Clearly picked out against the wall was an image of Julius, his face frozen into the act of a scream. Oh, my God. What were they doing to him to cause such pain?

Knees buckling, Adriel landed on the ground with a thump. Leith turned the air blue with language that proved no part of him could possibly be made up of angel.

"Are you all right? Adriel, answer me."

Words were stuck behind the lump in her throat. Whatever was happening to Julius at this very moment was her fault. Plain and simple. Tears ran unheeded down her face and dampened her collar. She had to do something to help. Talk about fight or flight responses; Adriel learned it was possible to experience both at the same time.

"I need to find Julius. I have to help him." Adriel scrambled back to her feet and began pacing around the tight space. Julius, in his role as her guardian angel, could locate Adriel anywhere in all the worlds, but her role as his charge canceled out that of being his trainer. She had no means for tracking him. Estelle would be no help in that department, either. The ability to locate a charge only went in one direction in order to keep the relationship professional.

"If you'll accept my help, I know a guy."

"A guy?"

"Faldor. If anyone could craft a way to track Julius, he can. There's a snag, though. He'd need something to serve as anchor for the spell. Angels don't have personal items, so I'm not sure how this would work." This was a side of Leith she hadn't seen before. The pragmatic, helpful side. Good to know he had layers.

Hayward house was full of things Julius had owned when he was alive. "Then we're in business because I've got that covered. We just need to go to Oakville. Do you have a car, or are you going to wiggle your nose and transport us there, Jeannie?"

"There you go again, mixing up the classics. Samantha wiggled her nose, Jeannie blinked like this," Leith folded his arms and combined an exaggerated blinking motion with a head bob. Despite the teasing words, the look he gave her contained enough surprise that it made her wonder what it was she had said to put it there.

"I've always wanted to go on a road trip." How long had Sylvie been standing there?

"The drive to Oakville probably isn't long enough to qualify as a road trip." Leith drawled. "Someone owes me a favor; I'll call it in for a pair of wheels. Give me a couple of hours, and I'll pick you up at the entrance to Tidewell Park."

Great. Two hours of Sylvie's voice buzzing through her head like an earwig. Adriel could hardly wait.

Chapter 12

"Whoa," Leith loosed a low whistle when turning the final corner revealed his first glimpse of Hayward House. "That's just…whoa. It's the house that Jack built."

The place often had that effect on people. The main body of the house started life as a perfect example of Greek revival architecture, complete with fluted columns holding up a pedimented roof over the front porch. By itself, that would have been eye-catching enough, but Julius had made some changes to adapt the structure to his tastes. A pretty penny he'd paid to convert the two wings on either side of the main house to something out of a Gothic fairytale. Spires shot into the sky above a pair of arch-topped windows exquisitely wrought in stained glass. A single tree mirrored in two seasons—summer and winter—faced the driveway. Their spring and autumn counterparts looked out over the grounds to the rear of the house.

Precisely manicured grass played against plantings of perennial flowers and marched between the driveway and the building that had once housed Julius' workshop, and later the museum Estelle had opened.

"It's the house that Julius built. Stay here. I'll be back as soon as I can." Injecting her voice with a commanding tone Adriel hoped Leith wouldn't question or argue. He had no idea the can of worms his presence would open should he accompany her inside. She had called ahead for just that reason.

It took all of two seconds before Adriel realized getting in and out of Hayward House quickly had been a fantasy. Lola rocketed around the corner of the house and made her customary beeline toward whatever humans had come to visit. Gangly as a newborn giraffe, the big boxer ran full out with a ridiculous doggy grin on her face. She might top out at close to a hundred pounds, but no one had ever been able to explain successfully to Lola that she was a big dog. Twisting her body and bouncing like a maniacal Chihuahua, she did her happy dance before slamming against Adriel's leg.

Leith, who had clearly ignored the order to remain in the car, slapped a steadying hand around Adriel's upper arm just in time to keep her from landing in a heap. The rapid motion pulled Lola's focus, and she stopped dead in her tracks, swiveled her head to pin him with a look.

What would the dog make of Leith? Getting the answer to that question almost made it worth bringing him inside. Almost.

On more than one occasion, the loyal dog had proved herself an impeccable judge of character. He stood still under her consideration while the moment drew out. Finally, she gave what was for her a delicate sniff—think huge sneeze with liberal amounts of drool—and pranced toward the front door where she issued two short barks. Status undetermined. Not helpful.

The door swung open to frame Julie, who clapped eyes on Leith and sealed the deal. The newcomers would be joining the entire group for one of Tyler's patented cookouts. Adriel readied herself for questions and winks and nudges. What was it about the happily paired up that made them think everyone else's life remained incomplete until they did the same?

"We don't have time for a party." It came out with a sharper tone than Adriel had intended.

Julie eyed the former guardian without the least ounce of trepidation, "This isn't a party, it's a strategy session. Julius means a lot to all of us, and you'll accept whatever help we can offer whether it's a place to stay, something to help track him, or another bout of ring around the Earthwalker. We're in." She waved a hand to indicate the entire group gathered on the back deck, turned and without looking to see if she was being followed, passed through the sliding glass doors. "And don't try any of that wrath of Adriel stuff on me, either."

Behind Julie's back, her husband Tyler stifled a smirk while he flipped burgers of both the beef and veggie variety with equal skill.

A knowing look passed between the four women. There would be some kind of discussion about Adriel's so-called love life—or lack thereof—before she could make her escape this day, so she decided to put an end to it before it started.

"This is Leith. He doesn't think I'm capable of finding Julius on my own." She tossed away his dignity without a second thought. "Leith, meet our hosts, Tyler and Julie."

The smirk on Tyler's face turned into an expression of choked back laughter as he waved a spatula toward Leith as a form of greeting. "Underestimate Adriel at your own peril."

"Where have I heard that before?" Leith's tone was dry.

Tyler waved the utensil again, and a drop of grease splattered onto the man busy shucking corn into a plastic trash can.

Finn Kent brushed at the tiny spot absently, his attention more focused on the woman standing next to him than on the new arrival. Who could blame him? His fiancée, Gustavia Roman, could distract a saint. Tall as a warrior, she wore a three-tiered skirt in pink, purple, and blue that fell to shapely, bead-bedecked ankles; a sherbet-orange tank top peaked through at least a dozen necklaces. Her wheat colored hair, in a feat of nearly impossible engineering, rose in an inverted cone-shaped arrangement almost a foot high and was festooned with tiny tassels. The woman was a walking cure for a bad day. Even a clown would smile just looking at her.

Adriel pointed to the couple and named them for Leith as hugged Gustavia. In awe of the vision before him, he stammered out a greeting.

Next in line for introduction was Gustavia's brother Zack, who leaned against the cedar deck railing, one arm casually slung over the shoulders of Kat Canton. The smile on his face appeared open and friendly to the casual observer, but anyone who knew him would see the way his sharp eyes, honed by years on the police force, assessed the new arrival thoroughly. Without mentioning the earlier close encounter, Leith assessed him right back.

"This is Zack and Kat, and next to them we have Reid and Amethyst."

Reid Grayson, the newest member of the group, towered over his diminutive wife, Amethyst who, other than being two feet shorter than them, would not have looked out of place among the three faeries Adriel had met this week. Sometime during the past few weeks, Amethyst had changed her hairstyle from a chin length bob to a charming pixie cut that only served to emphasize her elfin features. Decked out in her signature color of head-to-toe purple—including hair, nails, and lipstick, she stood eye-to-eye with her husband's shirt pocket.

Head tilted and a speculative expression on her face, Amethyst gave Leith the once-over, caught Adriel's eye, raised an eyebrow also dyed a delicate shade of lavender, and went back, no doubt, to assessing his aura.

The Earthwalker battle this past spring had had repercussions for several of the people standing on the deck—Amethyst's being the most dramatic. Going from someone with the ability to perceive auras to a Reader with a capital R had increased her ability at least tenfold. For a short while, the effects had been debilitating to the point where her friends had worried for her sanity. She'd come through the experience with super-enhanced levels of auric vision and a certain amount of healing ability.

Introducing Leith to her might turn out to be a good thing. Seeing auras was something Adriel could no longer do with ease. Knowing lies from truth—that she could still manage with somewhere near my earlier accuracy—and Leith had never lied to her, but Ammie would have a better handle on the intentions behind his truths. Unlike Adriel, she wouldn't be blinded by emotions she couldn't quite name.

When Amethyst finally spoke, the husky depth of her voice at odds with her tiny frame, it was in a tone even dryer than Leith's had been, "You're not normal, are you?"

An odd expression, somewhere between a frown and a grimace crossed his face. "Are you?"

"Oh, honey. What's the fun in that?" Amethyst circled Leith a couple of times, fingers twitching with the urge to play among and assess the shifting patterns of light she saw around him.

"Hear, hear." Gustavia grinned from ear to ear.

Judging by her frown of concentration, Amethyst was going to give Leith a thorough vetting and Adriel wanted a front row seat. She snagged a place on the bench, rested her back against the picnic table, and kicked her long legs out in front of her. Kat, joining Adriel a few seconds later, maneuvered her body into an identical posture and whispered conspiratorially, "You know that man is trouble, right?"

"Alert the media," was the sarcastic reply.

"What does Estelle say about him?" Since Estelle generally had an opinion on everything, it was a valid question.

"Not much." Estelle had been spending most of her time elsewhere, and Adriel found her lack of commentary troubling.

Kat, being sensitive, picked up the vibe and turned thoughtful.

"Anything from your spirit guides?" Since all Adriel's contact with anyone from home now ran strictly through Julius and Estelle, she was effectively cut off from most sources of pertinent information—a lack that left her feeling bereft of support at times and consummately annoyed at others.

"They're troubled but optimistic," Kat said unhelpfully.

To give him credit, Leith stood patiently while Amethyst scrutinized him thoroughly. Only once did his expression register surprise. Leaning in close, Ammie whispered something in his ear that made his eyes widen and cut toward Adriel, then quickly away.

When it was done, she gave him a pat on the arm and announced that he had passed.

Maybe now, Adriel hoped, they could eat and get down to business.

"I've been thinking ever since you called," Julie forked a bite of apple pie into her mouth and chewed with obvious pleasure before adding, "and I think I know just the thing to give you. You said it needed to be portable, durable, and something my grandfather handled frequently. My first thought was a piece of jewelry until I realized Julius didn't own any. Not even a wedding ring." That sounded about right.

92

"So, I went through some boxes in the attic and found this," she handed over a black, foot-long, fluted metal tube that had a point on one end and a ball on the other.

"What is it? His magic wand?" Leith's wisecrack was met with laughter, and Julie gestured for Adriel to hand it back. Grasping the ball firmly, she touched a hidden mechanism and with a ratcheting sound, the pointed end extended to triple its former size. It was a cane.

"One of his own creations. Do you think it will work?" Underlying the lighthearted banter, there were faint frown lines around Julie's eyes that testified to her worry on Julius' behalf. Since the tracking spell was Leith's idea, he was the one to answer.

"It should do." Briefly said, but reassuring.

Chapter 13

As they approached the space between two buildings, a shiver ran along Adriel's skin that had nothing to do with the cool breeze and everything to do with the field of magic running across the span. A shallow ridge of detritus had built up along the edge of the shimmering line as though mundane bits of paper and debris were barred entry to what lay on the other side.

Had Julius trustingly followed someone across a line such as this before he disappeared? Malachiel's gift had to do with the powers of persuasion; a glib tongue coated with sugar tempting his charges toward making the right choices, rather than providing the bare minimum of guidance needed for them come to decisions on their own.

An inexperienced angel would stand little chance of seeing through Mal should he choose to turn his focus from truth to lies. Even now, he could be urging Julius toward a fall. With that thought in mind, Adriel sent up a prayer for his protection, hoped someone up there was listening, and followed Leith across the line.

The shiver turned to an electric tingle that faded quickly but not before reaching the painful stage for half a second. Even the light looked different on the other side of the line. Gone were the buildings and the shadow between. Instead, Adriel found herself in the most unexpected of places: a carnival. Flashing lights, dinging bells, the cries of carny workers beckoning marks to take a chance, win a prize, guess your age. Come in, see the strange, the weird, the wonderful.

And beneath the frantic surface ran the feel of something neither dark nor light, but ready to jump at either. Magic.

"What is this place?" She grabbed Leith by the shoulder, pulled him to a stop to face her so she could better gauge his answer. "The Circus of the Damned?"

A quick grin lit his face. "No, it's just the Fringe."

That explained a lot and nothing at all. Of course, she'd heard of the Fringe—the name for the places where worlds bumped up against each other and overlapped—but she'd never had reason to visit one. The Fringe was forbidden to angels. Rules were being smashed just by Adriel being here.

Or were they? She hadn't followed a charge across the barrier, and having a physical body made her sort of human, so maybe there wouldn't be repercussions. The little voice of anarchy that rode around with her these days made a snarky comment about how she was pretty much on her own anyway, and so what if the Powers didn't like her every decision. It was too late to do anything about it now.

Moving forward determinedly to walk side by side with Leith, Adriel ignored the knowing grin that came from watching her wrestle with the decision to turn back or go on.

With the distraction of her swinging moral compass out of the way, there was room to notice all the strange things about the place. Despite the mix of realities represented and the frantic nature that went along with any carnival, the atmosphere remained decidedly low-key. Everyone who wasn't an angel seemed quite at home.

A pair of pointy-eared elven children sprinted past to take the last open spaces on a Tilt-A-Whirl with scarred seats and aged paint. Their shrieks and giggles as the relic spun them into the curves sounded no different from the ones Adriel would have heard in the world she was used to. She wasn't sure why that comparison fascinated her, but it did.

Passing through the midway, Leith and Adriel made their way up a gentle grade to where a series of buildings marched in rank and file along a curved path. When a brawny goblin lad led his two-headed goat toward a penned-in area behind one of the livestock buildings, she goggled like a tourist and Leith had to tug on her arm to get her moving again. The familiar smell of hay and manure seemed out of place here.

Beyond the agricultural section, the path trended downward at enough of an angle to reveal the peaked tops of more than a dozen tents running down each side. Compared to the giddy sights and sounds of the midway, this section seemed darker, almost sinister despite the brightly-colored awnings.

"This way." Leith's guiding hand burned Adriel's arm like cold fire, the sizzle reaching all the way to her toes, leaving a trail of gooseflesh along the way. She swallowed a gasp and acted like nothing had happened. His face gave away nothing of whether he felt the shock as well.

"What? You're not going to win me a stuffed animal? Those rainbow sparkled unicorns are cute."

He pretended he hadn't heard the muttered question, but a hint of a smile slid across his lips to leave as quickly as it had come as they made their way toward the business end of the carnival.

Crudely carved or drawn signs advertised the wares and services to be found inside the open tents or behind a closed canvas flap. For a few dollars, a person could learn their fate, find love, or purchase a weapon crafted by magical means. One tent was filled to overflowing with enchanted jewelry. Gustavia would have had a field day picking out bangles and baubles.

At the fourth tent from the end on the right side of the path, Leith paused. The sign in front carried nothing more than a carved symbol. A circle with a line bisecting it that ran from the two o'clock position through seven o'clock.

"Let me do the talking," Leith insisted.

He took silence for assent and half dragged Adriel inside. She knew the second her toe crossed the threshold this place held great power. The earthy scent of dried herbs filled the small, close space. The familiar thyme, mint, and rosemary competed with others she couldn't readily identify made her head spin for a brief second. A couple blinks cleared the miasma from her eyes, and she saw Leith already seated in front of a mahogany table with a scarred top.

"Sit down, Adriel." His voice was soft and encouraging, quite at odds with his usual brusque tones. "Our host will join us shortly. There's nothing to fear."

Easy for him to say. He wasn't the one flouting conventions just by being here.

Adriel's heartbeat clanged in her head with the sound of a thousand bells when she felt the newcomer's presence prickle across her skin. There went her chance at getting out of here without anyone from home finding out. All the air left her lungs in a whoosh of shocked surprise.

"Galmadriel."

"Lamiel."

Mirrored expressions of dismay showed on the faces of both angels.

On the short side, as angels go, Lamiel would have to stand on the second step of a staircase to look Leith in the eye. Expressive in their disdain, his dark eyes flanked a long nose with nostrils that flared as though he smelled something offensive. His lips were pressed into a straight line, and not a single mousy hair on his head was out of place.

Why did our civilized greeting feel like we just shouted en garde at each other? Adriel wondered. *We're on the same side, right? Or have I crossed over to the darkness without even realizing it?*

Her thoughts raced to the beat of her galloping heart until she heard Estelle's voice like a cold shower in her head, *pull yourself together.*

Swiveling in her seat, Adriel searched, but Estelle was nowhere to be found.

In the hierarchy of angels, Lamiel ranked below the council of powers and above the guardians which, in the past, had made him Adriel's superior. In the present—well, she didn't know where she fell in the rankings, but she'd lay odds on him being a thorn in her side.

"Interesting company you're keeping these days." The comment delivered in a mild tone was intended to put her in her place. It failed utterly. Too bad for Lamiel.

"I could say the same about you, Lamiel. If you have an opinion of me that you think I need to hear, then stop beating around the bush and speak right up." Prickles of otherworldly energy rippled and sang harmony with Adriel's displeasure. Even with her seated, Lamiel had to look up to meet her eyes. Whatever he saw there diffused his pique, and on a sigh, his face collapsed into lines of worry.

"You have no idea the wheels you set in motion with one reckless act."

Self-righteous fury melted into a puddle of pain. Everything that had happened—Julius being detained; darkness taking spirits out of turn; the impending doom of imbalance between the realms—was all her fault. Sickness swamped her belly, churned it to an acid volcano that erupted into an inner tirade. How could she have been such an idiot? An arrogant fool who thought she could act with impunity based on paltry millennia spent watching over humans. She was so busy berating herself, she missed half of his next sentence.

"...ever successfully banished an Earthwalker once it has taken a host. If you can teach us how to do the same, we have a real shot at keeping on top of things." Wait, was her mind playing tricks? Lamiel sounded excited and positive. What was she missing here?

Silence fell while Adriel played that question over in her head, and she didn't notice when Lamiel stopped talking. At least she managed to drag her mouth shut once she noticed it hanging open. Finally, on full alert, she eyed the parchment he'd laid on the table between them, a quill poised over it as though he planned to take notes. Beside her, Leith's shoulders shook twice, but when she looked at him, there was no sign of laughter.

"I...what?" No one was going to pin any medals on Adriel for being a scintillating conversationalist that day.

Leith rose from his seat. "I have some other matters to attend to, so I'll leave you two to talk." He was gone before anyone could say boo.

Lamiel's eyes narrowed. "Give me the step by step account of how you vanquished that Earthwalker without killing the host. Leave nothing out."

"Oh, you think it was me." His eyebrows shot up into his hairline before beetling into a frown.

"It *was* you." There was an element of question in his statement.

"I was merely the focus. It took an entire group of friends—mortals—to help me send Billy back to the depths where he belonged, and even then it was a close thing." Too

99

close, considering the way Kat had become lost during the skirmish.

Lamiel's swarthy face lost half its color. "Then there is no longer hope." With restless fingers, he rolled the parchment into a tube and stashed it in the folds of the cloak thrown hastily over his shoulders. "If you will excuse me, I must go." He made a move to stand, but Adriel had reached her limit. She stood abruptly, the force of her upward trajectory knocking the chair to the floor.

"You owe me the courtesy of an explanation." Being shut out of everything had taken a toll, but all of that was about to end.

To her surprise, Lamiel settled back in the chair, his eyes roved over her face appraisingly. "I suppose it cannot be helped. We believe Malachiel intends to turn an angel into an Earthwalker's vessel." Lamiel lowered his voice as though describing a secret scandal.

Playing it off as though she hadn't heard this theory before, Adriel gasped theatrically, "But, that would be..." The word stupid came to mind along with catastrophic, and several others that the angel in her wouldn't allow to pass her lips.

"Yes?" Lamiel waited eagerly for her response.

"Impossible."

"How so?" Eager interest pulled him forward to listen more closely.

"Light." A simple answer. "Light was the weapon we used to drive the Earthwalker out of Logan Ellis without sacrificing his soul. One moment of physical contact from me and there would have been an entirely different outcome." Adriel paused, took a moment to think through the repercussions of what had happened during those final moments of battle.

100

Darkness and light coexists inside each mortal in a dichotomy that forms the very basis of free choice. Billy's possession of Logan had pushed the needle almost all the way into the black. Working alongside Amethyst and the other three women, Adriel had created a field of containment and then fed the light of creation to the blackness lingering in Logan's soul. No dark creature could stand in the face of such glory, and the Earthwalker had fled.

The plan had been brilliant, if she did say so herself, and it had also been working perfectly right up to the point where the men had arrived to "save the day". Adding their light to the mix had pushed past the limit's of Adriel's control and once Billy was gone, the backlash of pure power arrowed straight to the clearest channel it could find, blasting straight through Kat and sending her across the bridge before her time.

"You want to hear the real cosmic joke?" A bitter laugh nearly choked Adriel in its way out. "I've spent my entire existence looking at humans as weaker beings who needed to be guarded from their own treacherous natures. We look down on them. All of us do. No, don't shake your head at me; it's true. We—I took pride in my role as a bringer of light, but when it came down to saving Logan Ellis, it was the humans who took the lead. I served as channel but they did all the work.

Julius will stand. If anyone should know that, it's someone like Malachiel who gave up his light to embrace the dark. Any attempt to force the issue will result in a stalemate at best, and destruction at worst," she explained to Lamiel.

She told him every detail, leaving out the part about how she'd realized her newfound mortality had come with a direct line to her shadow self, made her the only angel capable of carrying light while being susceptible to corruption. She supposed the news should have scared her. What it did was make her angry. Next-level angry. Red-faced, teeth-clenched, shaking with fury, spitting mad. Lamiel pushed back away from the table, a frown on his face.

"It seems you have come to the correct conclusion." His mild tone was meant to soothe and failed miserably. Adriel stalked back and forth the three paces the area allowed.

"I guess I have." She halted abruptly, then regained her seat. "I've told you everything." The very last, thing he had wanted to hear was that saving vessels required mortal assistance.

"Now that you know the whole story, you should also know that I have no intention of letting Malachiel plant a ticking time bomb in my soul. What could he hope to obtain by pulling a stunt like that?"

"That's what Leith has been helping us figure out." Lamiel leaned in to whisper, "Can we trust him?"

"How should I know? I only met the man two days ago," Adriel hissed back. "You're the one who seems all chummy with him."

"Yet my sources tell me you took him to see your *friends*," he spat the word out like it was a curse. "What does the reader say about him?"

That he has a nice backside probably wasn't what Lamiel wanted to hear, and it was all she could do not to snort when she imagined the look on his face if she said it. Romance had its time and place. This was neither.

"It's complicated." Understatement. "He has ties to the darkness, but it is not in him. When I met him, he was fighting for the light, protecting a spirit from darkspawn bent on taking it below." The image played back in her head. "Using supernatural means." Carefully deciding which section to show, Adriel projected the mental movie to Lamiel who watched with interest as Leith cast the energy ball at the reaper.

"See? He went to great lengths to protect Sylvie at the moment of her passing. It wasn't his fault she chose to remain behind." Was she trying to convince Lamiel or herself? Sighing, she showed him the rest of it. There was nothing else to look at in the stuffy confines of the tent, so when his eyes went wide, and the breath whooshed out of him at the point where the evil thing made contact with her wings, Adriel's eyes were trained on Lamiel's face. It took several minutes afterward to recover his composure.

"I know, I know. I'm not supposed to take my wings out in plain sight. Give me a break, though. I'm new at having them go all physical like that." A hint of a frown that he quickly smoothed away suggested Lamiel's thoughts ran in a different direction. A notion Adriel filed away to ponder later. Right now, helping Julius was more important than re-establishing her position among the host.

"Who are the powers sending in to help? Zekiel's good under pressure, and he has experience with taking on the darkness." Lamiel's face went so still it felt like looking at a mask.

"Zekiel is on assignment elsewhere." The long pause between question and answer said more than the words alone.

"No one is coming, are they? You and the rest of the Powers have decided to cut their losses and throw Julius to the wolves." To his credit, Lamiel had the grace to look down in shame. "Just like they did with me. Cowards."

Blood thrummed toward her head with pounding force behind the rage building up inside. "Thanks for all your help, Lamiel." Sarcasm dripped like sweet honey from Adriel's tongue, and if strong emotions had carried physical power behind them, the force of her anger would have made his head explode. A savage sneer curled her lip, narrowed her eyes. "Thanks for nothing, Lamiel. I'll show myself out."

"Wait." The inside of the tent lit with the sudden glow of Lamiel's will springing to life. He lifted one finger, circled it with such a precise movement, it was more a suggestion than an actual gesture. A heaviness fell over the two of them. "Listen carefully. All is not lost. You must trust that never will you walk alone."

"Spare me the platitudes. Next, you'll be telling me it's always darkest before the dawn."

"Isn't it? You'll need to play to your strengths," he gave her a pointed look, "your humanity and your allies will see you through." Even now, his nostrils flared at the mention of her group of friends. "Trust your instincts; they've taken you this far. You are in a unique position to take action in an area where we, your brethren, cannot tread nor can we openly supply support. There is more at play than you understand, and I regret that I cannot provide more illumination. Trust that you are not forsaken."

He could have sprouted a second head, and she would have been less surprised. It sounded like he had faith in her. Fancy that.

Speaking rapidly now, Lamiel added, "None of this is coincidence. You must have been chosen for this duty, no matter the evidence to the contrary. And for good reason. Look for Julius in the place where all power is equal. If you find him before the full moon rises, all will be well. You have a weapon Malachiel cannot fight because he does not truly understand loyalty. And for the love of the almighty, make better choices this time." Eyes burning like coals, Lamiel dispelled the shroud of silence, and with a sound like the ringing of a bell, was gone.

Slumping back in her chair, Adriel drummed fingers on the table and tried to make sense of his warning—if that's what it was. Time pressed in on her, pregnant with foreboding.

Her trainee was in more trouble than she thought, and each minute brought him closer to being beyond saving.

She took stock. She had no plan, no idea where to look for the place where all power was equal, the added burden of a wayward faerie, and a crew that consisted of people she'd prefer to protect rather than toss into the middle of an attempted coup. Saving Julius was turning out to be something of a fool's errand.

And Adriel suspected she was the Fool.

Chapter 14

Outside the tent, Leith leaned indolently against the side of a wagon that looked like it had come straight off the set of a movie about gypsies. A green roof arched over side panels painted in once-bright colors now faded to pastel hues. Patterned curtains decorated a pair of rounded windows. Framed by the deep blue-green trimmed door stood the most beautiful woman she had ever seen. Considering Adriel's age, that said a lot about the woman's beauty. Raven black hair fell in waves well past a nipped-in waist and contrasted with the dusky blush of her cheeks. Ruby lips pouted under the pert nose she was currently using to look down on Adriel with. When she wasn't watching Leith with possessive eyes and an aggressive stance, that is.

"Is this the broken angel?" The words were a sneer delivered in a language a hundred years dead.

"Better broken than twisted," Adriel replied in kind and watched those expressive eyes darken from deep brown to black under their fringe of thick and dusky lashes. Her pout turned into a hard smile, and she gave Adriel a grudging nod for speaking in her mother tongue.

Her haughty glance raked Adriel's form up and down in that way catty women use to wreck another woman's confidence. It didn't work. At all.

"This is Bianca." Leith's lazy drawl failed to hide amusement at Adriel's expense, and Bianca preened in a way that seemed as though hearing her name would mean something more than it did. When Adriel's expression remained remote and polite, Bianca's face darkened.

"Nice to meet you." Adriel reached out a hand in greeting, and Bianca navigated the steps with all the grace of a cat in predator mode, grasped the outstretched hand, and whispered, "You're too tame to hold his attention long."

Adriel flinched. Not at Bianca's aggression, but her own. Getting or keeping Leith's attention had never been part of her mission, and yet a spark of something akin to jealousy raged dangerously close to the surface. A little tingle of power shivered through the tenuous contact, and this time it was Bianca who flinched and tried to pull away. *Teach her a lesson*, a voice in Adriel's head commanded. *Give her a good jolt*. That voice had become a lot more vocal lately.

"Be nice, Bianca." The warning was delivered with an air of indulgence from Leith, then met with a sniff and a whirl of patterned cloth as Bianca mounted the steps, cast one furious look over her shoulder, and slammed the door hard enough to set the wagon's springs creaking.

Beckoning to Adriel, Leith held out a hand, which she ignored for a long beat. He met her steady gaze with a smirk, then turned toward the midway and left her standing there without a backward glance. She was tempted to stand there until he had gone.

Instead, she dawdled along behind him and examined her hostile reaction to Bianca's challenge. An eternity spent in the service of humans, and she had never realized how intense was the pressure of temptation they battled. No wonder free will was such a big deal. Concentrating on the nature of her human side's baser instincts let her ignore, at least for a few minutes, the cause for them.

107

Jealousy. Really?

An expensive emotion and one she could ill afford given her dual nature and ethical responsibilities. As long as the tiniest smidgen of angel remained, indulging in a relationship with a man would be just wrong. All kinds of wrong.

Leith was more than just a man. By that token, maybe he didn't count. There was that little voice again, talking nonsense.

As if he knew she was thinking about him, he slowed until Adriel caught up and they continued walking side by side.

Adriel pushed all thoughts of relationships far down into the deepest reaches of her psyche before they posed more temptation than she could handle. Even the most fleeting of accidental touches, like when his arm brushed against hers as they walked, was enough to transform her pulse into a raging beast with a craving for more. He excited her in ways she only understood from a thousand lifetimes of watching people but had never experienced herself.

She wanted more. Almost as much as she wanted to breathe, and all the while knowing *more* had as much potential to bring her life as it did to be the death of her.

"Adriel."

Leith's voice penetrated deep thoughts with the impatience of someone who was becoming tired of repeating himself.

"Wake up." His fingers snapped just ahead of her nose.

"What?"

"We're here."

"We are? Where's here?" She looked up to see they were standing in front of the entrance to the mirrored depths of the Fun House. "You're joking. Tell me you're joking."

A wide grin split Leith's face. "You're not claustrophobic are you?"

"Of course not." Okay, maybe a little, but only because small places weren't built for someone with wings. Or invisible wings, at any rate.

Confined spaces made Adriel's back twinge with the effort of keeping them folded tightly enough not to catch on anything. Even when they were tucked away, she felt them like phantoms. According to Amethyst, people with tall auras are uncomfortable in low-ceilinged rooms, so it might not be totally crazy. "Lead on."

Bare-bulb carnival lights lined the pathways between mirrors, their reflections creating a disco-ball effect as they repeated from one side to the next. Dust lay thick along the edges of the path Leith chose, his steps following no deviation. He knew exactly where he was going.

Two minutes in, Adriel was sure this was no regular funhouse attraction. Amid the standard mirrors that warped her shape from tall and thin to short and wide, were some that offered more. She passed a parade of the various bodies she had taken on in the course of her guardian angel duties.

Goth girl with her jet-black hair and makeup morphed into a plain-looking woman in her mid-forties who peered over a pair of half-rimmed glasses. A little girl with pigtails and overalls grew into a grizzled woman with a kindly face. Leith sped up his pace and the next image Adriel saw was a weary-eyed woman covered in scars and tattoos that quickly altered into a fifties housewife complete with a bouffant hairstyle and a twin-set sweater.

She was zigzagging down the last series of rows before it occurred to her that looking at Leith's images might be enlightening. Without seeming to, Adriel sped up just enough to catch a glimpse. At first she thought the phenomenon only worked on angels because Leith looked exactly the same until, in the next to last mirror, there was a slight difference. His eyes glowed with liquid fire.

Trying to see his hidden persona had distracted Adriel from noticing that even as she sped up her steps, Leith had done the same, and by now we were right on the edge of running. The path widened out, and the mirrors on either side turned to clear glass that showed the sides of a long tunnel.

"Hurry, or we won't make it." Leith grabbed Adriel's arm and sped into a dead sprint. Her long legs had no trouble matching his pace as they raced for the doorway ahead. She chanced a single glance back and saw that behind their fleeing forms, the lights set to illuminate the path were dimming, one after the other. If they didn't hurry, when the last one went out, they would be plunged into complete darkness.

That final minute stretched out long amid the sound of pounding feet and labored breathing. The pair hit the end of the line just ahead of the fading light, and Adriel's heart dropped like a stone. It was a dead end. She balked, but Leith's inexorable grip pulled her forward on a collision course with a thick glass wall separating them from the mouth and the light at the end of the tunnel.

She hit the glass at full tilt and, to her amazement, slid right through with nothing more than a faint tingling sensation to mark its passing. The momentum carried them into watery blue daylight, feet pounding a fair way down the cobbled street before losing momentum and slowing to a walk.

"Where are we?" Somewhere she probably wasn't supposed to be without express permission from the Powers.

"Does it look like Kansas, Toto?" If the grin was supposed to soften the mocking tone of his voice, or worse, be considered charming, it failed harder than Pepsi Free.

"Ha, so funny I forgot to laugh. Where are we?" Thatch-roofed cottages with stucco walls in faded blues, pinks, and yellows lined both sides of a narrow thoroughfare.

"Plausible deniability, Adriel. If you don't know, you never have to admit to being here. Fifteen minutes is all we need. You still have the item with you, right?"

She pulled the telescoping cane out of my pack and held it out for him to see. "Of course."

"Come on, then. Let's get this done." He started off down the deserted street and, wondering where all the people were, Adriel followed. One thing was for certain, they were not in any part of the mortal world where she had ever been before, and since there was no such place, it stood to reason they must be in another world entirely.

At the fourth cottage on the right, Leith paused and cast a sober look her way. "You should probably let me do the talking. Faldor can be a bit touchy sometimes. And whatever you do, don't stare at his nose. He's sensitive."

"Okay." Adriel shrugged and followed him through the door. The charming cottage-style exterior could not have been more different from the cave-like interior of the house. Directly opposite the door was a fireplace large enough for a grown man to stand up in without fear of knocking his head against the flue. The soot from a thousand fires darkened the walls in an ombré effect that started out black near the cavernous hearth and lightened to a steel gray around the entrance door.

Hanging over the fireplace was the trophy head of an animal Adriel couldn't quite identify. It looked like Howdy Doody and a buffalo had a baby. Shaggy ginger fur covered a narrow, sloped forehead that really didn't go with human-shaped ears the size of dessert plates or the short horns that curled out low on either side of a lightly-furred face. It even had freckles. Fascinated, Adriel looked around the room a bit more. Bunches of herbs dangled from heavy wooden rafters and perfumed the air with pungent, earthy scents. Adriel counted fifteen different sizes of mortar and pestles arranged on tiered shelves to her right. The shelves looked like they had been built by someone who had refused to read the directions because from where she stood, each one was slightly askew.

A bank of mismatched cabinet doors ranged around the room leaving only space for the fireplace and a doorway that led to what she assumed was a sleeping area beyond. A scarred table with a thick top that had been fashioned from a single slab of wood took up most of the room's center. Half the table was covered with tightly stoppered bottles full of liquids of various colors, several of which glowed with their own light.

"Faldor," Leith roared, "Haul your sorry carcass out here. You have guests."

"Smooth," Adriel commented dryly and received a gently-placed elbow in her side as a response.

"You bring me what I asked for?" The voice that emerged from the back of the cottage was deep with an accent that sounded faintly British. "I don't work for free."

From some hidden pocket, Leith pulled out two bottles of pale amber liquid and set them on the table hard enough for the clinking sound to carry through the doorway. Beer? The wizard worked for beer.

Faldor strode through the door and despite her assurance to Leith, Adriel couldn't help but stare at his completely unremarkable nose for a few seconds. He returned her perusal with a sardonically-raised brow.

"You have got to stop doing that." Faldor warned Leith with a cheerful grin.

Apparently, Leith's sense of humor had stopped maturing somewhere around age twelve. Faldor was made to blend into a crowd of bankers. Average height and build with mouse-brown hair. Wire rimmed glasses perched on a nose that would not draw a second look. The only thing that stood out in his face was the merry twinkle in his eyes.

"He does this every time he brings someone here."

Leith let out a barking laugh. "You should see your face."

"You should grow up." Adriel extended her hand to Faldor and said, "I am Adriel, pleased to meet you."

"Likewise." Faldor ignored the outstretched hand—she was beginning to sense a trend; no one in this realm wanted to shake hands—traded an oblique look with Leith, and gestured toward one of the chairs circling the big table. "Did you bring the item?" He reached over to twist the top off one of the bottles, and as he did, he turned it so Adriel could see the label. Cream soda. Tipping up the bottle, he swallowed the entire contents in three big gulps, belched, and wiped a hand over his mouth. Adriel bit her lip to hold back a smile.

Reaching over her shoulder, she pulled the compacted walking stick from the side pocket of her pack. With a flick of the wrist, two hidden sections telescoped into place, and all it took was a twist to lock them. She laid the cane on the table.

"Will this work?"

Faldor lowered a hand to hover over the cane and closed his eyes.

113

"Hmm. Yes. A strong personality. Stubborn. Creative. Passionate. This will do nicely. Give me a minute to compose the proper ingredients."

Leith pulled two more bottles from another secreted pocket, and Faldor's grin widened. "Ah, sweet nectar." A lascivious look plastered itself on his face, and he reached for another bottle.

"Spell first, drink after," with a quick hand, Leith slid all three out of reach and earned himself a dirty look, but Faldor nodded agreement and began to bustle about the room pulling from various shelves a series of ingredients.

A stone mortar and pestle landed on the table along with a fistful of herbs.

"Grind those to paste," Faldor handed Adriel a bottle full of pink liquid. "Use this. Just enough, you'll know when it's right." He assumed a lot, but she set to with a willing hand. When she cracked the seal on the bottle, the scent reminded her of the flowers in the fields back home. A homesick tear trembled on her lashes until she dashed it away. There was no use in crying over what she could not control.

Faldor grabbed the mortar and dumped the contents into a small cauldron suspended over the fire. Adriel watched with fascination as he muttered to himself while selecting items to add. A gallon of water followed the herb paste into the pot and then, of all things, an old shoe.

"For distance," the wizard announced.

A pencil landed in the pot with a rattle as it hit the sides. Faldor had tossed it from atop a short stepladder. Almost faster than the eye could track, he crossed the room to open another cabinet and pull out an old battered compass. "For knowledge and direction. And this last is to bind the spell to you." On his way back past the table, he seized several of Adriel's hairs and yanked them out of her head.

"Ow." It popped out before she could bite down on the exclamation.

The hairs went into the pot, and a puff of smoke rose from its depths. Faldor seized the cane from the table, ran it through the pink and roiling cloud.

"Quaere Veritatem," Seek truth, Faldor intoned three times. The cane lit up pink for a moment before returning to normal. He handed it back to her. "It's a single use spell that will work across worlds and will last for no more than three hours. Speak the owner's name three times to trigger the spell. I wish you luck," and with a smooth motion, Faldor snatched a second bottle of cream soda from the table, popped the top, and slugged it down. When he set the empty container back on the table, it was with wobbly hands. If she didn't know better, Adriel would swear he was drunk.

A questioning glance at him had Leith confirming that she actually didn't know better. "Sugar and carbonation. He'll be too wasted to talk if he drinks all four."

Stowing the enchanted cane back into her pack and saying goodbye elicited nothing more than a flicking motion of Faldor's hand as he tipped up bottle number three. By the time Leith and Adriel reached the bottom step, she could hear his voice warbling a semi-incoherent song extolling the pleasure and the pain of drinking too much.

"Interesting company you keep," she said to Leith.

"Faldor's all right. He only goes on a bender once or twice a year. His spellcraft is solid, though."

Faster than she would have expected, they arrived back at the tunnel entrance. From this side, no glass barred them entry; only a shifting curtain of wavering light arced across the mouth.

"Think good thoughts," Leith warned and then pulled her through before she had time to think any thoughts at all. The curtain briefly fell around them like a waterfall, but she felt no lasting ill effects from it. Leith, on the other hand, spent the next minute bent double and shaking as though from fear.

"Are you okay?"

"Fine. You didn't feel that?" Envy wove through his tone.

"Feel what?"

"Never mind. A goody two shoes like you wouldn't have had any wicked deeds in her past to feel guilty over."

Adriel glanced behind her, but the curtain was gone. and the glass had returned. By the time she turned back, Leith had recovered himself and, brushing off all inquiries about what had just happened to him, urged her to follow him back the way they had come. Somehow she got the sense that this mission had cost him more than four bottles of cheap soda.

Chapter 15

The night of the full moon loomed, and Adriel was no closer than before to solving Sylvie's murder or having a concrete plan for saving Julius and Vaeta. Weighing one mission against the other left her in no doubt which she would choose if it came down to it. Vaeta, by all accounts, had chosen to give herself to the darkness, while Julius had not.

What she needed was a devious mind.

What she needed was Estelle, who hadn't been checking in on anything like a regular basis.

That was about to end. To call Estelle to her, Adriel injected as much force into her voice as she could and spoke the errant guardian's name aloud. Once. Twice. Three times. Not because there was some inherent magic in the number three, but because Estelle had been scouring the city for any sign of her partner, and that was how long it took her to get from there to Adriel. Come on. She's not Beetlejuice or the Goblin king or anything.

Ariel held her breath until Estelle finally appeared. The first sign that Julius had fallen into trouble was his failure to respond to her calls. She worried Estelle had been taken as well.

The air shimmered like a mirage and disgorged the newly minted guardian into Adriel's borrowed living room. Estelle looked flustered.

"You have news." A sigh of relief.

"I do. Just give me a minute, and we'll talk."

The unholy beast of a coffeemaker beeped to let her know she was supposed to pull one of the handles or something. Undoubtedly the manufacturers intended the noise to be a helpful alert, but Adriel found it more of an ominous warning sound that bad coffee was about to happen. Since bad coffee was better than no coffee, she braved the hissing behemoth and was rewarded with a cupful of bitter brew. Estelle took a chair at the table and watched with fascination while her mentor poured half a mug, filled the rest with a combination of water and creamer then dumped in a ponderous amount of sugar. She declined Adriel's offer to turn solid and partake of a cup. A sensible response.

Taking Lamiel's cue, Adriel dropped a cone of silence over the tiny house and repeated what little information he'd been able to provide. She saved the bombshell of Malachiel's ultimate goal for last and kept mum on the notion of whether he was the genius behind the scheme or merely a pawn in a bigger game.

"That's why they've shut me out." As soon as the words were out, Estelle clapped a hand over her mouth.

Adriel put on her best teacher-to-student glare. Estelle squirmed but spilled her guts. "Right after we rescued Craig from Malachiel's influence," Estelle referred to Pam's uncle. Preying on the man's guilt, Malachiel had used him as a battleground for the first skirmish. It had taken an expedition into Craig's mind to free him from the fallen angel's influence. "I went back to report to the Powers. I thought I could get them to see reason—to understand how they've tied your hands by saddling you with me. They're the good guys, right? It's their job to send the cavalry."

Estelle had a lot to learn about the inner workings of the power structure she was now part of. The intricacies surrounding free will could be limiting at times, and yet, they were necessary to maintain the delicate daisy chain of balance between good and evil.

The Powers would act against anything that threatened free will, but they took their sweet time deciding between what constituted a threat and what was a mere consequence of actions. Their job was a difficult one, and Adriel freely admitted there were probably a million things the Powers must consider in any given situation.

Angel 101. Help. Guide. Protect—and most importantly, allow your charges to make their own choices whether you agree with them or not. A thankless job most of the time, and yet Adriel missed it like she would an amputated arm. Her work was a source of ultimate sorrow and consummate joy— often at the same time.

"This was during my missing time?" Estelle's eyes dropped for just a fraction of a second. She knew something about where Adriel went in the time between missions and had either been ordered—or was choosing—not to tell. It was a fifty-fifty shot for which option ticked Adriel off the most, but she let it go. For now.

"Looks like we are the cavalry." A bitter twist curled Adriel's lips. "Best we get down to it." She pulled what she needed from the desk drawer and wished she had one of those whiteboards with the erasable markers. In the old days, she could easily have called one to her, but that was then, and now there were limits. Estelle wouldn't graduate to that level for a generation or three, so a pen and a pack of rainbow-colored pastel sticky notes would have to do.

Jotting furiously, she created a timeline for everything that had happened since she landed here.

"Sylvie's murder is the priority." Not least because the chatty spirit had taken to popping in frequently to get updates on the case. Adriel jotted down the meager information Zack had given her. Sylvie's boyfriend, Dante, had alibied out with an ironclad story. Officially, he was off the hook, but Zack still considered him a person of interest.

She went over everything piece by piece with Estelle for the next hour or so.

"How do you feel about doing a little undercover work?"

"Just tell me what to do, boss."

The undercover work Adriel had in mind skirted the gray area of the rules—a shade she had become intimately acquainted with in recent days. Technically, asking Estelle to spy on Dante went over the line since he was not her assignment. Someone would probably receive a reprimand. Probably not Adriel. This fell into throwing someone under the bus territory.

"Before you agree, you should know you could get into trouble with the Powers for what I am about to suggest." Warn first, throw second.

"Just tell me what to do."

Adriel did and sent her off with Sylvie the minute the young woman's spirit made an appearance, then returned to her makeshift evidence board to look for clarity. Until she felt the cooling wetness on my cheeks, she hadn't noticed the frustration-fueled tears spilling across them. Infinite—well, until lately—experience as a tool for the Almighty left her unprepared for becoming a finite creature with dreams, desires, and fears. Right now, it was the latter that weighed on her. Scrubbing at the wetness with the back of her hand, she added several more hastily scribbled flutters of yellow to the wall. Extending the timeline back to when Cassandra had her first experience with soul-stealing darkness, Adriel chose green notes for all the information the oracle had provided, which added another dimension to the whole, and a pattern began to emerge. One that turned Adriel's guts to ice and had her scrambling for the purple pack of notes and then the blue.

By the time orange and pink filled in the blank spaces, her motions had turned robotic. Write, turn, stick without hesitation. She could have stopped long before finishing because there was no need for the rainbow of color to show her the way anymore. She knew exactly what she was looking at.

All of it. Or almost all of it. There was one wild card still in play that could change everything.

Leith.

Shock buckled her knees so hard she barely made it to the sofa where she sank down to wrap her mind around this new set of truths and steel herself for what was to come.

Chapter 16

Estelle's return with Sylvie served as a welcome distraction right up until the reluctant ghost refused to discuss her boyfriend, Dante.

"He's not my killer. Why can't you just leave him alone?"

As gently as she could, Adriel explained, "He's a person of interest and might have useful information. The kind that would help us catch whoever did this to you."

Sylvie refused to budge on the topic, and instead, pelted the angels with questions about what would happen if she didn't get to go into the light.

"We're doing our best to make sure that doesn't happen."

After exchanging a telling glance with her trainee, Adriel sent Sylvie off to visit Cassandra. The second she was sure the ghost had gone, she turned to Estelle and said, "We need to talk."

The words no more than left her lips when an unearthly shrieking noise filled the room.

"What the…" It was coming from her pocket—given the force of her emotions, it was probably the death knell of the little phone—and just when she had started to trust that her energy field had settled enough to stop interacting poorly with those little chips inside it. The phone caught the edge of the pocket when she tried to yank it out, and the force spun it out of her hand. The device hit the floor hard enough to send the battery in one direction and the back panel skittering under the table.

The noise continued unabated.

Estelle put on her physical form and scrambled for the phone parts while Adriel searched her pockets for the source of the racket and came up holding the little seashell Evian had given her. Apparently, this was the Fae's way of reaching out and touching someone. As soon as Adriel lifted it to her ear, the din subsided to be replaced by Evian's voice. Something akin to panic turned her normally dulcet tones strident.

"You are needed." The shell shook hard in Adriel's hand, and she pulled it away from her ear just in time to avoid being drenched. Water flowed from the shell as though through a hose and formed itself into an undulating globe that hung in the air like a mirror or a window. An image quickly formed that showed Evian and Terra kneeling next to the prone form of Soleil as she lay on the floor. Evian turned, her gaze taking in Estelle's presence and noting her solid form. "Hold tight to the shell, take Estelle's hand, and walk into the water. Hurry."

Adriel traded a look with Estelle, who shrugged, but did as Evian asked. The bubble turned out not to be a door at all. As Adriel stepped into it, her head spun with the sensation of being enveloped by the water and tossed into a maelstrom of motion. Think of it like a genie flowing back into her bottle, and you'll get the idea. Estelle and Adriel were sucked into the shell, which returned to Evian's hand and then spewed them out again in a liquid rush. A most unsettling sensation quickly forgotten in the somber atmosphere hovering around Soleil.

Instead of landing in Evian's underwater grotto, Adriel found herself standing in a well-appointed foyer. A crystal confection of a chandelier hung overhead and cast gentle light over the grim scene below.

Worry hung over the room like a dense cloud, getting heavier each time Soleil took another labored breath. Adriel fell to her knees beside Evian while Estelle circled to kneel next to Terra, who held both hands over her sister's heart. "What happened to her?"

"I came back from a work thing and found her like this." Tears ran unheeded down the young woman's face. "She's barely breathing. Somebody do something."

The stories you've heard about faeries being the next best thing to immortal are mostly true. They age about a million times slower than mortals and aren't especially easy to kill. It can be done, though. Soleil was about to become proof of that unless someone did something, and fast. Her face was already turning gray.

"What can I do to help her?" Adriel had no idea—this was her first time having more than casual contact with any of the Fae. Healing had been one of her duties as a guardian but was more complicated than just laying on hands and saying poof; you're all better. The healing had to be sanctioned from higher up. Plus, the person had to believe, had to want to be healed—and not just with their heads, but with their entire being. There had to be a bigger lesson in the healing than could be learned from the affliction. Even then, a guardian could only give the human a push; they had to do the work on their own. Just another facet of free will.

Face pale enough to make her eyes look like sunken stones; Terra spared Adriel a glance. "She's fading, and I don't know what to do."

"How long?" Adriel had an idea.

"An hour, maybe a little more."

Not much time, but it might be enough. "Can you send one of those portal things to someone who doesn't have one of your tokens in their possession?"

"Not really, but if they're near a large enough body of water, I can cast a scrying onto it. I just need to know the location." Maybe a visual link would be enough. It was worth a try.

Adriel pulled out her phone, hoped it still worked. Tension slowed her fingers, fumbled them over the keys, and she felt her heart sink when the screen flashed from red to blue to green. Apparently, it was a mood phone from the eighties. When she got nervous, upset, or anxious, that's when it turned unreliable—and at the moment, Adriel was all three of those things. There wasn't time to explore the ramifications, but she made an effort to calm herself, and the screen returned to normal.

Amethyst answered on the third ring, and Adriel took no time for formalities.

"Are you home? Alone?"

"I am, but if you ask me what I'm wearing, I'll freak out and hang up." Humor lightened Ammie's unnaturally deep voice.

"Funny. Go down to the lake, please. I'll stay on the line."

"Good for you, but I won't. There's no service down there." Because that would be too easy.

"Just go, then. And don't be scared."

"Why, what's going to happen?" Adriel heard the door slamming behind her. Amethyst trusted me that much.

"I promise, you'll know it when you see it." The phone beeped to signal the lost call, and the line went dead. She gave Evian the coordinates, and it took a moment before a pane of water-made glass shimmered into view. Another frantic series of motions, and there stood Amethyst. Close enough to touch, but not really.

In as few words as possible, Adriel explained the situation to the wide-eyed aura reader.

She gestured toward Soleil. "Can you see her? Her aura? Something happened to her, and we're hoping you can give us a clue by reading her energy field. She's dying." That last statement was unnecessary; Amethyst had already figured out that much based on nothing more than her initial glance at the situation.

"Can you all step away from her so I can see more clearly?"

They did as she asked and Adriel heard, rather than saw, Amethyst's quick intake of breath as the image before her became more clear.

"Oh, my. That's...I've never seen anything like it."

"We're running out of time here. If there's something you can do, then get on with it." The room shook from the force of Terra's booming growl.

"Adriel, come around to where I can see you." Adriel complied.

"There's nothing around her body, but at about here..." Amethyst held her hands less than a foot from her own shape. "I see light in shifting reds and oranges that seem to be seeking her, but when the energy gets close, it disappears completely. Not like it is fading out, but like it is being cut off. I think she has a force field around her. Something." Amethyst's attention focused on something behind Adriel who turned to see Evian looking thoughtful.

Amethyst continued, "You, there." She pointed at Evian. "She's like you, right? Your aura flows toward you, not away like ours do. Can you explain that?"

Evian's mouth rounded in surprise right before her eyes narrowed, "Aren't we perceptive?"

126

"Getting snippy with me after you've asked for my help is counterproductive. If you want to save your sister, you'll tell me what I need to know."

Shoving at her sister, Terra fixed steady brown eyes on Amethyst. "We are elementals, which means we pull our life force—what you would call a soul—from the elements that form our nature. My life comes from the earth, Evian's from water, and Soleil's the sun."

Taking that explanation in stride, Amethyst and Evian came to the same conclusion.

"Something is blocking her from her element."

"She's starving to death."

The two spoke at the same time, their voices triggering in Adriel a memory of her wings becoming a physical shield and shredding the darkness as it closed in on a helpless, newly-formed spirit. A similar action might work here. The only questions were whether she could consciously call them into being—that time it had happened during a moment of pure adrenaline-filled terror and if her wings would work the same way in this situation as they had in that one.

"It's a long shot, but…" There was nothing to be lost from trying. Sooner rather than later, judging by the lengthening space between Soleil's fluttering breaths.

Taking a moment to center herself, Adriel pulled the sense memory of that moment back to the surface. The stretch and burn in her shoulders as the feathery weight tugged at muscles unused to their burden. The lightness in her soul when the slightest down sweep battled gravity for a split second. The white light of them. The smell of purity. The clear notes of air whistling across their surface at each movement. The ache in her soul at the thought she might once again test their strength on the wind's current and soar.

So real was the memory Adriel could have sworn they'd sprouted from her back. When she opened her eyes, it was to know the crushing disappointment of failure.

"Don't just stand there, do something," Evian ordered.

"I'm trying." Another thought, this one not remotely pleasant. What if Leith's presence had been a factor? Given Evian's temper, Adriel was less than sanguine about the Fae's willingness to expose her family to him. But if it was the only way, she'd have to come around.

"Estelle, can you find Leith and bring him here." Without letting him know our location. That last part conveyed through mere thought. Estelle returned a look that Adriel had trouble reading but winked away to do what she was told.

As expected, Evian protested. "Right, why don't you just bring in the National Guard?"

"Do you have a better idea? You asked for my help, and this is the best I've got." There was more heat in Adriel's voice than she intended, but it wasn't her fault her life was in a state of flux, and there were still some of her abilities that came and went without rhyme or reason. If the people in her life would stop having a crisis a minute, Adriel thought she might find the time to devote to regaining control over her skills.

Estelle was gone no more than five minutes, each one feeling like an hour in the heavy silence broken only by sighs and quiet sobs. The charged atmosphere must have communicated something of the gravity of the situation to Leith when he swirled into the room in a rush of dark leather and the heavy scent he carried with him. Brimstone. What had he been doing? Or maybe Estelle had taken the time to fill him in. Either way, Adriel laid out the situation for him using terse words and humbled herself enough to ask for his help.

128

"Can you remember anything from that day that might help me now? Something that might trigger my instincts?"

Leith raised a sardonic brow. It was the only motion in an otherwise still body and said more plainly than words he was in one of his supercilious moods. The man had more of those than a woman riding the PMS pony.

"No need. I'll take care of it." He knelt down and reached toward Soleil. "You're out of your league, little angel."

Adriel had heard of people seeing red; it's just that up until that moment, she thought of it as a metaphor and not an actual possibility. It turns out she was mistaken. Pulsing red flooded her vision as her blood boiled hot and made her forget she had asked for his help, to begin with. She slapped his hand away. Hard.

Even if he could be useful, the bit of hubris humanity called an ego wouldn't let Adriel back away to see him try. It was tempting, though. After all, if he failed, she could gloat. She wasn't proud of the impulse. That Leith had supernatural powers was not in question; his intentions were. For all Adriel knew, he could have been the one who put the whammy on Soleil in the first place.

Leith's smirk at the sound of Adriel's flesh sharply meeting his pushed her over the edge.

Distracted by the satisfying mental image of flaying him to the bone, she stopped trying so hard to manifest wings. That, coupled with a heightened desire to protect Soleil pulled out of her what no amount of wishing or will could have done. Adriel's wings unfurled in a blaze of white-lighted glory and cocooned over Soleil to break the force of darkness surrounding the prone faerie. She began to stir just as Leith whispered into Adriel's ear, "See? You just needed to get all riled up and then get out of your own way. It's sexy."

Adriel's burning look failed to blast him to bits in any real capacity. Worse, he reacted by patting her arm and grinning at her as if she were a kindergarten student who had just managed to print her name. The man was insufferable, and the place where he touched her arm only tingled because she disliked him so intensely. Or maybe because he had some level of power at his beck and call. It could not be attraction. Angels don't feel those kinds of emotions; only humans do.

Right.

With the danger over and the adrenaline ebbing from her system, Adriel waited for her heartbeat to return to normal, but before it could, the slamming of a door set it galloping again.

A lilting voice called out, "I'm home. Where is everyone?"

"In here." Evian tossed a pleading look Adriel's way. "Please don't tell her what happened." Estelle faded from view but remained close.

"You'll never guess what…" Adriel's first impression of the woman behind the voice was of barely-contained energy. She was dressed in business casual—the dark skirt slitted to allow a hint of knee paired with a fitted white blouse seemed severe in contrast to the brightly colored scarf knotted carelessly around her neck. Dark hair curled to gently frame lively eyes the color of a blue jay's feathers. "…happened?" Concern finished the sentence with a question as she took in the somber faces turned her way.

"Nothing. Everything is fine." Soleil's voice sounded tired still. "We have guests."

Evian handled the introductions somewhat curtly by pointing to them in turn. "This is Adriel and Leith." She pulled the young woman in for a one-armed hug. "I'd like you to meet Alexis."

130

"Lexi," Alexis corrected with a long-suffering sigh. "It's Lexi. How do you know my godmothers?"

Godmothers? They were faerie godmothers? Too funny.

Something of her amusement communicated itself to Terra who flashed a dirty look and then it was Adriel's turn to be dismayed.

"You know you're soulmates, right?" Lexi pointed to Adriel and then to Leith, who looked away so fast Adriel couldn't get a peek at his reaction. "Trust me; I have a sixth sense about these things."

The wheels turning in Adriel's head finally clicked into place.

Faerie. Godmothers.

Protectors of witches in much the same vein as she had been a guardian to mortals. Terra gave a barely perceptible shake of her head, which Adriel assumed meant she should keep her mouth shut. A moot point since she was too flabbergasted by Lexi's comment to say much of anything anyway.

Leith, however, was not.

"See there; I told you we were meant to do great things together."

Adriel's answer to that was a withering stare that he ignored completely, instead choosing to turn his charm on Lexi by according her a courtly bow. "How perceptive of you."

"Not really, it's kind of my thing. I have a knack for putting couples together."

With Lexi's attention focused on Leith, Adriel signaled Evian with her eyes and said, "You have a lovely home, I'd absolutely love a tour of the place." It could have been a grass hut for all the attention she'd paid to the place up until now.

"Of course. Let's start in the kitchen."

Keeping up a descriptive patter, Evian led Adriel down a short hallway with several closed doors leading off of it and into a room lit by a bank of windows. With stainless steel commercial-grade appliances, miles of maple cabinets polished to a gleam, and floors tiled in glittering granite, the kitchen lived up to my chance comment. Reid and Amethyst's little house would have fit in the space where the table sat with room to spare. Faerie godmothering must pay a lot better than guardian angeling.

They circled an island workspace toward the front of the double-door refrigerator situated in the farthest corner. Once out of Lexi's hearing, Adriel hissed, "How powerful is she?"

"Whatever do you mean?" Terra feigned innocence. Badly.

Adriel folded her arms, tilted her head back, and surveyed the water Fae with narrowed eyes. If Evian lied now, she was done. "Three godmothers? She, herself, is either dangerous or she's a target for someone who is. Remember who you're talking to. I know how these things work." In theory, anyway.

"A little bit of both, okay? Look, Lexi isn't a factor in this whole thing with Vaeta if that's what you're worried about." Adriel searched both face and energy for signs of a lie and came up empty. "It's under control."

"How much does she know?" Not that she expected to spend any amount of time with Lexi, but being armed with enough knowledge not to shove her foot in her mouth at some point seemed like a wise decision.

"Lexi is the last in a powerful line of blood witches with a history of the type of dysfunctional family values that ends up being featured in horror movies. She is aware of the basic facts and that her knack for matchmaking is witch-borne."

"Then Leith and I..." Adriel closed my eyes to let the implication sink in.

"A fated match. Lexi is never wrong." Not the news Adriel wanted to hear, but there is a first for everything, so she held onto that hope as they rejoined the others.

"It's time to go." Before he had much of a chance to protest, Adriel dragged Leith out of the house and down the street—full speed for several minutes before she realized she had been too preoccupied to figure out where she was. For once, Leith had the sense to remain quiet. That lasted about a minute.

"You're going the wrong way."

Taking a second to orient herself, Adriel realized he was right, and kept going anyway.

"Why do you act the way you do? You talk about us being together as destined, and then the next minute you act like you think I'm a child—or worse, an idiot."

Laughter belled out of him, rich and deep and toe-tingling. "Keeps your ego in check."

Laser beam eyes, that's what Adriel would want for her superhero power if she could have one. Her regular ones tried to burn a hole through the arrogant jerk. "Or does it keep me from asking too many personal questions?" Adriel caught the tiny motion when his shoulders twitched. Score one for angel insight. "Tell me how you came to be the defender of innocent souls."

The pause that spun out between them lasted so long Adriel thought he had chosen not to answer, and then Leith said, "I only exist to do this work."

His words tasted of truth, and of doubt, and of something unexpected. Sadness.

"Believe it or not, I understand."

"You might be the only other person on the face of the planet who could," he admitted ruefully. "We have a lot more in common than you know."

Before she could ask what he meant by that, Estelle showed up.

"You're going the wrong way," she said helpfully and followed with raised eyebrows when Adriel growled at her.

"How can that be possible when I haven't decided where to go next? Just tell me that." What she wanted most was an hour of alone time to think, and plan, and just be. Embarrassing as it is to admit, the only thing that had been standing in her way lately was herself. Half her angel assignments had consisted of popping in at the right time to give someone the message that self-perception could be either a stumbling block or a stepping stone. Excellent advice, even if it did sound like a platitude. The kind of advice that seems fairly obvious when you're not the one on the receiving end of it. Duh.

Believe to achieve is the basis of the self-help movement, and Adriel had been the one to deliver that message in the first place. Humanity could thank her later.

Tuck your tail between your legs and slink away before you get any deeper into the power struggle between light and dark. The little voice in Adriel's head warned. It was probably the voice of common sense if she was honest.

"…our next move." Adriel only caught the last half of Estelle's sentence.

"Right," she agreed, and the next thing she knew Leith's hand landed on her arm. He made the transfer to the house on

Canal Street between one breath and the next. If there was one power Adriel wanted back; the ability to move between places was it. Hey, if he could do it...

Chapter 17

In the end, Adriel chose not to tell Estelle everything. Rushing in ahead, she hung the painting back on the wall to cover up her patchwork of sticky notes. Leith managed a fleeting look, but not enough, she hoped, to put it all together. More proof was needed before she was willing to involve the people—and angels—she cared about in something that could turn them into targets—or worse, into collateral damage.

Shamelessly raiding Reid's desk, she tossed pen and paper onto the table while describing the salient points of her conversation with Cassandra, and then they got down to business.

"Based on the oracle's description, I think we're looking for a nexus."

"A nexus?" Estelle said. "But how? They're just waypoints between worlds. Like a revolving door, right? The nearest one to here is three hundred miles away." A frown furrowed her brow, and Leith shifted in his chair.

"Is there something you want to share?"

"Wait, you haven't heard the story of the darkest heart?"

"That's a fairytale, nothing but a local legend."

Tilting his head, Leith scoffed at Adriel. "Oh, come on. You know every fairytale has a truth at the heart of it. Just because the bards put a good spin on their stories doesn't mean some of the events didn't happen."

"Would one of you please enlighten me? I haven't heard this one." Estelle could have pulled the knowledge from the source, but that was a skill she was still working to master. Adriel waved a hand to let Leith know he should do the honors.

"Once upon a time…" He began.

"Really?" she said.

"Just kidding. Rumor has it that a supernatural beast with the heart of darkness plagued the area until a prison was built to contain the threat."

"What does that have to do with Julius?" Estelle said.

"I believe Leith is saying that the legend is true, the prison is contained within a nexus which is located nearby, and he suspects Julius has also been imprisoned there. It's a total fantasy."

Adriel's vehement statement struck Leith funny. At least a minute passed before he finished hooting with laughter. Not even her sternest glare had any effect on him.

"I fail to see the humor."

"Oh, I know you do. That's what makes it so hilarious, but trust me, it's the only thing that makes sense." Leaning back in his chair, one ankle resting on the other knee, Leith smiled. "One day I'll let you in on the joke, but for now, let's keep our eyes on the prize."

That little voice in the back of her head said something scandalous about her eyes and his prize, but she ignored it. This was not the time for those kinds of thoughts. As if he had read her mind, Leith let his smile go a little wider and turn slightly feral. Every thought flew out of Adriel's head for half a second and then dropped back with crushing weight.

"Let's say you're right. Do you have any idea where the nexus is, or how to open it—assuming it's sealed."

"Sure." Leith sketched a rough outline of the city limits and added a few reference points. "This area, just off Market Street." He drew an X over the spot. "This is the epicenter of a disturbance that extends a couple of blocks in every direction." He corrected himself, "Not a disturbance exactly, more like a quiet exodus. This whole section of town is empty."

"Empty?"

"Right. Stores, homes, the whole nine. But that's not even the weirdest part." He leaned forward conspiratorially. "No one seems to have noticed. People just avoid the area, but no one talks about it. If there's something big and bad in the neighborhood, that's the place."

"Right. I'll go take a look and report back." Estelle left in a flare of light.

"It's not going to work," Leith's voice deepened. "Because I'm not letting you go alone."

He must have read her mind. It usually takes two to open a traditionally-sealed nexus. Since she technically qualified as both dark and light, Adriel figured she could probably pop this one open all by herself. No one else needed to be put in danger, and if she played things correctly, she might be able to stop this whole fulcrum business before it got any worse.

"At what point did you get it into your head that I need either your permission or your protection?"

"You'll have the one, but never the other. You think I can't see the wheels turning in that pretty head of yours?" Rising abruptly, Leith stalked to the wall and lifted down the painting covering the notes. "Or read between these lines?"

138

Adriel moved to stand beside him. "If you really do see what I'm seeing, then you know what I have to do. I won't let you stop me." The simple truth, spoken firmly. Nothing he could say or do would change her mind.

Not even what he did next, which was to pull her into his arms and kiss her until she felt like she was on fire. He swallowed her squeak of surprise and then Adriel was kissing him back. Deep, drugging kisses that stole her breath and sent tingling sensations screaming from her toes to her nose. How long it would have lasted, was impossible to say, but what stopped it was the sound of Estelle pointedly clearing her throat.

"When were you going to tell me about this?" She asked.

"It just happened. It's not like I knew you were standing there." Adriel thought she meant the kiss. Probably because it was all she could think about at that particular moment.

"Not that. This." Estelle pointed to the wall.

"Well, I started to tell you right before Evian called, and after that well, things got weird." Adriel felt like a kid caught with her hand in the cookie jar—and wasn't she the trainer here? The one who was supposed to be in charge?

"You give me your word right now that you will not do anything stupid. Right now, Adriel, I mean it." Estelle gave just enough of a push that her will tingled through Adriel like fire. Whatever intentions she had of sacrificing herself without endangering anyone else washed away. Estelle would stick like glue if Adriel didn't agree now.

"Okay. I promise not to do anything stupid." At least she hadn't specified what she meant by stupid, and when the two of them finally left her alone, she moved forward with the non-stupid parts of her plan.

It took almost two hours of concentrated effort to regain full control of her wings.

Something of Cassandra's prophecy came back during the sweaty effort.

Seek not your grace in the faces of others, in the wheels of time, nor mourn for its passing and home. Tis not gone, nor does it lie in subdued slumber. Tis not diminished by circumstance or flesh.

By circumstance or flesh. Flesh or circumstance. Flesh *was* Adriel's circumstance at the moment.

Embrace your path and that which blinds you to your own light will fall away. All that you have ever been or will ever be lies within you now as it always has.

A fancy way of saying what had already been said by others yet Adriel had not completely accepted. Earthbound and an angel still. That was her.

She reached for her grace.

Sweat pooled at the small of her back, dripped down her face, and dampened her hair by the time the motions had become smooth and effortless. Curiosity got the better of her in the end, and she lifted one of the mirrored closet doors from its track, propped it against the opposite wall, and angled it so I could see what happened to her clothes when the wings unfurled. That was a waste of time because it happened so fast she couldn't figure out the sequence of events, but best as she could tell, the wings morphed right through her blouse like it wasn't there.

The next skill to work on, she decided, would be the one most useful to her. If Leith could bend space to move between one place and another, then so could she.

Touching her grace came easier now; it had been a lack of focus and hauling around the extra weight that kept tossing a monkey wrench into the works. One measly inch was the best she could do before she fell face first onto the bed and was asleep before her nose touched cool cotton. It was a start.

Chapter 18

An insistent knock on the door disrupted Adriel's muttering and pacing: two very important pursuits that were keeping her from leaving right now to go singlehandedly pull Julius' fat out of the fire. Well, that and her promise to Estelle, plus Leith' threat.

"Adriel, open up." Julie Kingsley's voice echoed through the steel-clad wood.

"Come on; we're loaded up out here." And Gustavia's.

Adriel opened the door to the pair of them, plus Kat and Amethyst. Each of the four women carried an overnight bag in one hand and a food-related item in the other. Two boxes of pizza, wings, soft drinks, wine, and ice cream. The minute the door swung wide enough, Adriel was gently shoved out of the way as they swarmed in to drop their burdens and distribute hugs. It had all the earmarks of an invasion.

"Finn took Sam to visit her grandparents for the weekend; Zack is out of town for a seminar on something boring to do with a new fingerprint-reading app; and their husbands," Gustavia waved a finger toward Julie and Amethyst, "are absorbed in some online gaming thing that involves loud shouting of the word "booya" a lot. Hence..." she waved a hand again, "here we are."

"Hence?" What a load of hooey. Did they think Adriel couldn't see the looks passing between them? Gustavia was right up there with the top ten worst liars in the history of ever. They were here to a) take Adriel's mind off tomorrow's mission and b) horn in on same. She didn't have to ask how they knew. It had to be Kat.

"Hence. We needed a girl's night anyway, and we figured you could use the company. There are rules." Arguing with Gustavia, Adriel knew from experience, was like trying to unscramble an egg—a useless waste of time, and probably why they had made her their spokesman. One by one, each woman contributed a rule.

"No brooding," Kat intoned.

"Well, there go my plans for the evening." It was a joke. Honest.

"No dwelling on things that are in the past." That one was Gustavia's contribution and delivered with finality.

"You have to tell us all about Leith." Amethyst waggled her eyebrows. How did she know there was anything there to tell?

"And no telling Estelle any juicy secrets I might reveal." Julie grinned. "We promise, it will be fun, what do you say?"

Last time Adriel shared food and a bottle of wine with them, she'd gotten drunk off half a glass and accessed her body-morphing ability—something she hadn't been able to do since—and she had tried. As for tonight, there seemed to be little choice in the matter. They were here, and the distraction would do her good.

"Okay." Adriel tried to make it a statement and not a question, though it came out sounding like both. Ten minutes later, she was glad for the company. Warm laughter and the heavenly scent of reheating pizza filled the room. Julie and Amethyst did impressions of their husbands scratching sensitive areas and playing video games that had the others roaring with laughter.

The wine bottle made a single round, and Adriel abstained in favor of iced tea. A headache last time taught her a lesson about angel metabolism and alcohol that she planned never to repeat. Bright chatter soothed edges made rough by worry about things to come and glossed over the way Adriel had little to offer to the conversation. Too many topics were off limits in her capacity as not quite human.

Childhood stories require a childhood, which was something she had never experienced first hand. Very little of her past was open to discussion, and she feared her interpretations might be met with a lack of understanding. Not scorn, that was not the way these women viewed the world— even the stories they told about bad relationship experiences were tinged with gentle humor and self-deprecation.

An angel's life simply had not resembled anything they would understand and only now was Adriel beginning to find deeper meaning in the mortal world view. But, she did have questions. Particularly about Leith and the feelings he stirred within her.

"...so he puts on the sweater that's already covered in socks, and that's when it turns into a game. How many static-filled items can he stick on it at the same time." Amethyst screamed with laughter at the memory. "He's so caught up in it that he doesn't hear me come home and when I walk around the corner, I catch him with eight socks and two pairs of purple panties stuck to his chest while doing the most ridiculous dance to see if any would fall off. I'm laughing so hard I'm crying before he turns around, and when he does, he freezes like a deer in headlights."

"Tell me you had your phone. That was a Kodak moment." Kat wiped a tear of laughter from the corner of her eye. Not a year ago, she would have had to rely only on her imagination for the mental image, but tonight Amethyst pulled out a slim phone encased, naturally, in purple chrome and handed it around. Reid, a handsome man, wore a black sweater dotted with several purple items and a startled expression.

"Oh yeah, I made it my wallpaper. You'd think he would be embarrassed, but after he got a look at the photo, he decided to go for the record and added two more socks and a thong." Love for the man turned what could have been a mocking tone into one filled with affection.

"Leith kissed me." The words rushed out of Adriel in a blurt and elicited a chorus of woo noises and low whistles. "And I liked it." More whoops and whistling. Her face burned red. The irony of it all was that in her infinite lifetime she had less experience in this one area than the typical teenager, and right now that was exactly how she felt. Like a callow youth in the throes of her first crush on a bad boy.

Once the initial excitement of the revelation died down, Gustavia did what she did best and empathized. "You've never been in a relationship, have you?" Adriel's blushing face answered for her.

"Oh, Adriel. This has to be such a culture shock for you. Don't rush into anything unless you feel ready." A warm hand reached out for comfort. The simple affection conveyed by nothing more than a gentle touch undid Adriel and triggered a watery smile.

"My first kiss was the scariest thing I had ever done." Kat confided. "I felt like I was going to either throw up or burst into song. I didn't dare to open my mouth for at least a minute afterward because I couldn't predict what was going to come out. And then you know what I did? When I finally got my wits halfway back together, I burst out laughing. It was a nervous reflex." Her smile was part rueful, part nostalgic. The memory had not scarred her for life. Adriel's next breath came a little easier.

"Johnny Silverman. At a school dance. He smelled kind of salty and smoky at the same time. Our noses bumped, and my mouth went dry. The music just disappeared, and my ears started ringing, my heart pounded so hard it hurt. To this day, I judge every kiss by that one. Your first kiss is special like that. No matter how many come after it, you'll remember that one the most." Gustavia went all misty.

"Tell us." The gentle order in Amethyst's husky voice was both beguiling and conspiratorial. "I promise you'll feel better."

"Well, we were fighting." A look passed between the others that Adriel didn't understand. "What? What's that look about."

"Some of the best kisses happen during fights. It's all about the passion and the fire." A collective shiver ran through them. "And then the makeup sex." Just when Adriel's face had begun to cool, it flared hot and red again. Ignoring that topic seemed prudent.

"We were toe to toe and yelling at each other, and then we were kissing. I don't know how it happened exactly, but his breath was warm, and his lips were soft, and my body went all tingly. It was…" she broke off to choose the right word out of the handful that leaped to mind, "…exciting and scary."

"If it wasn't, you weren't doing it right." Gustavia hit on the one tiny point of fear Adriel had been keeping locked down deep. Becoming a person, a mortal, a human—and she realized these words were woefully inadequate in their ability to convey the most accurate description—meant so much more than just becoming a being of flesh and bone. Adding in a few angel bits made her existence an order of magnitude more complicated. Learning to pick her way through the minefield of what her inner angel was compelled to do and those things that meant living up to the demands of her new flesh was going to be an ongoing experience.

Woman. That is what she was now. A woman who has some fancy extras, but then again, what woman doesn't? Moreover, she was one who had missed all the rites of passage along the way. No wonder she was so confused.

Looking around the tiny table where the five of us were crammed together, Adriel sent up a prayer of thanks for these women who cheerfully accepted the role of guardian...hmm...humans? Persons? What term would sound less condescending? Gustavia would say Guardian Goddesses—in reverent capitals—but Adriel thought maybe that would be skirting the line a shade too closely. Mentors might work, but the word lacked a certain panache.

When the correct term came to her, she felt a little teary. A single word, both simple and eloquent. Friend. They were her friends. Lamiel had hit that nail squarely enough. Friends and that was no small thing. It was everything.

The barrier Adriel hadn't realized she'd been holding between them fell with a crash and a smile and a sense of connection that eased some of the raw places that came from feeling like something *other than* compared to everyone else.

The grin swept across her face like the tide rushing over the sand.

"Oh, I think I did it right. When it was over, he looked like he'd been hit with a stupid stick. There might even have been some drool, just there." She lifted a finger to indicate the corner of her mouth. Her flippant comment raised some eyebrows before the peals of laughter came. It soothed something savage inside her to feel like one of the group. For once she didn't have to moderate her tone to one more befitting her station and keep her inner smart (word she was not allowed say but means the part of your body you sit on) on the leash. The freedom almost took her breath away.

146

After the laughter and high fives, things turned a little more serious when Kat said, "You've never...um...you know." It was her turn to go red-faced until Adriel caught on to the meaning behind the question and became her blushing twin.

"What? No."

"So Angels don't...you know?" Julie said.

Adriel opened her mouth to say that was privileged information and nothing came out. Angel filter strikes again.

"But you could now if you wanted to." It was half a question and half a statement.

"Presumably. My body works just like yours." The need to change the subject was becoming a physical ache, so she turned the spotlight on Julie and felt no shame for doing it.

"Are you and Tyler planning on starting a family soon?"

"Not just yet. We're still newlyweds. Let's put in a movie." Julie deflected adroitly, pushed back her chair, and tossed the empty pizza boxes in the recycling bin. Adriel's ploy had worked.

Kat pulled a stack of DVDs out of her bag and the four of them clustered around her to choose a title.

"Practical Magic." Gustavia plucked it from the pile and popped it in the player before anyone else could argue.

"Hah, told you so," Kat chortled as Amethyst pulled a crisp ten dollar bill out of her pants pocket and handed it over amid more laughter from the group.

"Did I miss the joke?" Adriel frowned.

"That's right," Julie mused, "you were never there when these two made one of their infamous bets. See, Kat always knows, and Amethyst can't say no to a wager, so at least once a week she loses ten bucks to Kat."

147

"One of these days, I'm going to put one past her." Amethyst fumed, but in a cute and friendly manner. "Hey, is there any popcorn?"

"It's your house." Adriel teased, "How would I know? I have hardly had time for more than a shower and sleep. Thank you, by the way, for being so generous with me. I'm not sure the Powers understand my sudden need for things like food and lodging and those pesky personal hygiene products. They bounce me around willy-nilly without regard for my altered physical status." The bitterness she had been struggling against since the moment she realized what had happened to her could not stand against the common sense reason for actions she tried to view as callous disregard. How could those who had never experienced living in a physical body understand the intricacies of daily nuisances like smelly armpits, hairy legs, and greasy hair?

"Ask Estelle to explain it to them. And just know that anytime you need this place, it's yours. I can have a key made for you if you like."

That bit of overwhelming kindness made the decision Adriel had been wrestling with for the past hour go much easier. She would not risk her friends with this rescue business, no matter their arguments to the contrary or how valid their reasons for wanting to help. In the morning, she would sneak out early and leave them behind. Considering she was the reason Julius had gotten himself into this mess in the first place, Adriel would be the one to see him safe.

"Thank you for the kindness."

"It's nothing. You're one of us, now. Family."

Family. Loved. Accepted. Included. Trusted.

Undeserved considering she intended to betray that trust within the next twelve hours.

Family. Forgiven. She hoped.

Chapter 19

The first rays of sunlight glittered off a cloud of pre-dawn mist as Adriel let herself out of the tiny house with all of her meager belongings in a pack on her back and an enchanted cane in her hand. If she died today, she would leave behind nothing more than these in the way of worldly possessions. That, and the friendship of the women asleep in her temporary home. Safe. Right where she wanted them.

Turning her back on the faint light of the eastern sky, she pointed her feet south and west. She would have to pass through the heart of the city to get to the deserted section where Leith reckoned held the portal where she hoped to find Julius. If there had been a reason to doubt his speculation before, it was gone now. Firmly connected to her grace, the angel inside sensed the gathering darkness like a compass sensed true north.

This early in the morning delivery trucks ruled the streets, their wheels rumbling over pavement used to a heavier load of traffic, their exhaust pluming out to replace the oily perfume scoured away by night winds.

Farther on, Adriel's feet carried her through the arts district where each window displayed color and shape that provided a little solace to the soul. The yeasty scent of bread floated out of a hole-in-the-wall bakery to twist at her empty stomach, and the siren call of pecan rolls drew her inside.

Preparing breakfast in a roomful of sleeping women would not have been particularly stealthy.

Sugar, nuts, and cinnamon-laced bread filled the physical emptiness; a foam cup of steaming coffee warmed her stomach—but nothing could tame the wild ache of betraying friends. Even if it was for their own safety.

The cell phone in her pocket made a sound somewhere between its normal ringing and that made by a deflating balloon. Garbled text filled the screen to prove her emotional state was still capable of wreaking havoc. Instead of a phone, she carried a personal electronic mood-detecting apparatus. Thumbing the kill switch, she doubted that would be enough to stop the effects, but it was the only option.

Sending Billy the Earthwalker back to where he belonged had taken more energy than any single angel commanded alone. It had taken the combined effort of herself, two ghosts, the four women she had just left sleeping, and their mates. Now she was headed into an unknown situation with only Leith and Estelle on her side. Not great odds.

Adriel had no idea what brand of demon she might end up facing, and if there was one thing she could count on it was that the Powers would not be sending backup. She was looking at something between an epic victory and a suicide mission with no idea which she would be walking into. *Valid points of logic*, her brain whispered, *so why don't you turn around*? Her feet carried her inexorably forward.

When Evian shimmered into step beside her, Adriel should have been surprised. She wasn't. Somewhere in the middle of the sleepless night, hindsight had kicked in with perfect clarity.

"The Powers sent me here to do a specific job—make sure Sylvie crossed over. You called me back to the city that second time and let me think my assignment was Vaeta."

"So what if I did? I needed your help, and you need mine. Ours." Her sisters abruptly appeared beside her. "It's all connected. Sylvie, Julius, Malachiel, Vaeta. Would you have helped us without thinking it was a prime directive?"

"Do you have any idea of the consequences of your actions? I'm off book now. Maybe forever if the Powers decide I've gone rogue."

"Give them a little credit for knowing the hearts of their own." Terra admonished.

"Are you so sure they have your back?" This from Soleil. "They seem quite willing to leave Julius to his fate. Why are you so anxious to appease a group who cares so little for those they are sworn to protect that they allow human pawns to be the fulcrum point for the balance between light and darkness? It's like letting babies play with fire." Scorn dripped from her tongue.

"Remember the first time we met when I warned you about underestimating me? The same goes for mortals. You think your ability to outlive countless generations of them gives you more wisdom than they possess; that a shorter life span makes them powerless and weak. Forgive me for saying so, but you are arrogant beyond measure."

Soleil drew herself to full height and prepared to argue the point, but Adriel cut her off before she could utter the first word. "Extended life dulls all sense of urgency; makes you slower to recognize threats and respond accordingly."

"Did you just call me old?"

"Yes, and hidebound along with it." Adriel heard a snort from one of her sisters.

"That's...it's..."

"True is the word you're looking for," Terra observed dryly. "Don't forget, sister mine, how rarely we associate

151

ourselves with normals, and even the talented ones we choose to spend time with are of the long-lived variety."

Blood witches age at least ten times slower than the average person.

Adriel changed the subject. "How did you know where to find me?" She hadn't talked to the three sisters since helping Soleil, and that was before Leith identified the general area where Julius was being held.

"We've been tracking you all along. For your safety, of course," Terra said in a matter-of-fact tone that carried not the slightest iota of apology. Adriel's eyebrows felt like they might bounce off her hairline if they went any higher.

"How?"

"Trade secret." Evian refused to budge from that answer. Trade secret. Right. Stupid seashell.

While they walked, the sun burned off the residual mist and the city's heartbeat slowly increased. Traffic began to snarl the narrow streets and sidewalks filled with people rushing from home to work. Each step took them closer to the danger ahead and adding the faeries to the mix altered the plans Adriel had made with Leith, who should already be in position by now. Estelle would have to warn him.

"We should probably go incognito," Evian pointed out The next thing Adriel knew, three sets of tiny, winged creatures had taken to the air surrounding her head. It didn't escape her notice that their minute size presented a smaller target. At times like this, she missed being able to take incorporeal form more than ever.

Chapter 20

If her instincts had voices Adriel's would have been shrieking like a fire alarm in close quarters. Some places only exist behind a curtain of shuddering darkness, even in broad daylight. Without conscious thought, people detour around these areas until they fall into complete disuse—not quite forgotten, but barely remembered.

Julius' cane quivered in her hand, then pulled her closer to one such place. A narrow alley formed the entrance to a section of abandoned buildings one street over from busy Market Street. Something of her sense of purpose must have translated to the hordes of bargain shoppers clogging the sidewalk given the way they parted before her, almost without thinking, and certainly without reacting.

A tall, fiery-haired woman with a fierce expression on her face, carrying a cane she clearly didn't need, and surrounded by what probably looked like three dragonflies should have drawn a bit more notice. Adriel quashed the impish temptation to break into song just to see what would happen but allowed a grim smile to curl her lips at the mental image.

Maybe in time, she'd get used to the entirely human urge to run away from those situations her angel side was sworn to confront, but today the duality of her nature was very much in evidence. Dark energy flooded her being, brought the desire to turn her steps away, but she continued down the alley to the end.

All the sounds of bustling traffic muted from one step to the next as they passed onto concrete cracked and heaving from neglect. It was as if the city had forgotten this dead and broken place existed. Or maybe they were all too aware of its seething nature and hoped that, by attrition, the entire block would fall.

Sunlight dimmed here, almost as if someone had dialed back the wattage—yet, even in the shadows the air was heavy, close, and dankly humid. Adriel's nose wrinkled at the corrupt and fetid scent rising from the musty ground. Brimstone, maybe. Mixed with something equally black and toxic. Her footsteps sounded like muted echoes with hollow tones.

"Creepy." Hearing Evian's voice at normal volume coming from her minuscule form brought another fleeting grin. Too much Disney must have created silly expectations of her sounding like Jiminy Cricket when she was about his size. Adriel agreed with the sentiment, though.

"This way." The cane tugged at her hand just as a shout erupted from behind.

"Adriel, wait."

Oh no, what were they doing here? Adriel turned to give the four women hurrying down the alley her best stern look. Not surprisingly, it made no dent whatsoever in their resolve.

"I told you I would handle this."

Amethyst waved a dismissive hand at me. "And we said we wanted in."

"It's dangerous," she countered.

"It's Julius. Angel or ghost, he matters to me. To all of us." Julie said simply, her tone brooking no refusal. Stubbornness must be an inherited trait in the Hayward family. "We're coming with you."

154

Tempted to petulantly inform them it would be on their heads if anyone got hurt, Adriel would never voice the lie. Not only because lies were forbidden, but also because she already carried the blame for his being captured, to begin with. Every single step on the path that had brought him to this place—and the need to find him—had been taken at her direction. "Give me a minute to think." Adding an aura reader as strong as Amethyst to the mix could tip the balance more in our favor, and with Kat's psychic tracking abilities having been honed by working with the police, there might be a better way to mount this rescue mission.

Julie and Gustavia carried heightened empathetic responses, which had played a larger part in vanquishing Billy the Earthwalker than even they realized, but Adriel had no idea if there would be any use for them here. The Fae buzzed with muted opinions all the way back away from the alley, past the line of no return, where the noise from the crowded street could cover the sound of voices as they discussed a new strategy.

Estelle, Adriel called out mentally, *warn Leith we've suffered a series of complications.*

What kind? She replied

Fae for one, your granddaughter for another. Can you think in frustrated tones? It would seem so because Adriel did.

On it, came the faint reply. *You'll keep my Julie safe.* Not a question but an unnecessary order.

The delicate problem lay in mounting a sneak attack with five women, three faeries, a magician, and a guardian angel in training along for the ride. Worse, without reliable advance information, the whole contingent could be marching into a trap.

However, Adriel was not without certain resources. Chiefly, a vast range of secondary experience. Centuries spent watching over humans as they prepared for war had given Adriel tactical perspectives which she now used to assess her troops. She paired up a faerie with each woman based on their complementary areas of expertise. Evian and Kat were best at divining; they would handle threat assessment and early warning.

Terra and Gustavia, who, despite her appearance, was a grounded and level-headed thinker, would play rear guard. Julie's connection to Julius by blood made her an ideal secondary link to him in case the cane failed. Adriel assigned Soleil to her for protection and hoped she wouldn't regret the choice.

When Estelle returned, Adriel put her together with Amethyst, an easy decision. Estelle's common sense combined with the aura reader's abilities made them the best choice for shielding the group. Close contact with Amethyst, who could read energy signatures with ease, would only increase Estelle's reach. The trainee was about to have her strengths tested with a walk through the fire.

Leith, if he could be trusted, was already in place and Adriel would walk alone for reasons she chose not to share with anyone.

As for a strategy, there a vague, but basic plan. If that went south, they would have no choice but to play it by ear. So little of their intel came from trusted sources that the best plan was to stick together, assess the situation on the fly, and hope to keep Leith as their ace in the hole.

This time when the group strode out the mouth of the alley, it was with enough purpose to create a wind in the hair moment. Okay, so it wasn't the first time Adriel had tried to have one of those and failed. Last time the wind ignored her because she lacked a physical body. This time, it would have been more powerful if the air hadn't been so heavy that it plastered the titian strands to her head. *And, you know,* she thought *if the underwire from my bra wasn't poking me in the armpit.*

They kept up the breezy pace for half a block before the whole thing started to feel a little silly. Terra was the first to spot Leith's signal. If she hadn't been paying attention, they might have missed it entirely. Amid a wash of dirty graffiti just above eye level on the concrete wall of an abandoned dry cleaners was painted a star-tipped fairy wand. How droll.

Every few seconds, the wand turned to an arrow, then quickly regained its former shape.

That was the cue. Adriel gave Estelle the signal to snap her energetic tether onto the three faeries, who abruptly vanished from sight—each taking the woman she protected along with her. One by one, Fae protection spells slid into place, and even the slight rustle of their clothing fell silent. A tiny shell braided into Adriel's hair—courtesy of Gustavia's deft hand—would be her only means of communication until it became necessary to drop the shields. She tapped the shell twice to activate it, and their voices returned. When it was all over, maybe she'd tell Evian and the others that the shell made them sound like munchkins from the Wizard of Oz movie. Maybe not.

The cane in her hand twitched twice, then tugged sharply forward, and she followed, her invisible entourage no more than a step behind. The dark area remained confined to a two-block radius, on that point Estelle was certain, yet the empty street between here and there appeared to stretch out long. An optical illusion or a bending of the laws of physics, Adriel couldn't tell, but she walked for what might have been miles or only yards before the cane jerked again in her hand.

"You're being watched." Soleil's voice sounded loud and strident as she made the pronouncement.

"Thanks for the update, genius." Terra chided. Adriel could almost hear her eyes rolling in their sockets. "Any other blindingly obvious facts you'd like to comment on?"

"Hush," Estelle commanded. "You're acting like children."

"She started it," Terra muttered.

They were going to get everyone killed if they kept up their bickering.

The breeze from them reached her a split second before the sound of fluttering wings shushed in Adriel's ears. Malachiel waited. Black pinions stretched fully across the two-lane street to brush feathery tips against the brick and mortar walls on either side.

"I'm here for Julius, Mal. Make it easy on yourself and let him go without a fight." Fairness dictated she offer him a chance, even if he chose not to take it. Besides, who was Adriel to rob him of his villain moment? You know the one, where the villain is compelled to talk about how bad he is and why he did what he did. It usually comes right before he makes the stupid move that enables the hero to take him down. Encouraging him to speak his piece worked in with her goal of distracting Darkwing while the others carefully picked their way beyond him to where the cane indicated Julius was imprisoned.

Covering her actions by brushing away an errant strand of hair tossed into her eyes by the breeze Mal's wings generated, Adriel triggered the second gift the faeries had given her. A gentle tap activated the tiny crystal tucked into a crease near the corner of her eye and glued on with eyelash adhesive—Gustavia carried half a makeup aisle in that purse of hers. The faeries and their human companions snapped into warped focus. An odd sensation, Adriel's right eye saw only

Mal and the empty street stretching ahead of and behind him, while her left revealed a more interesting sight.

Terra tossed a saucy wink over her shoulder and, grasping Gustavia's hand, sank below the surface of the soil which parted beneath them as if it were water. Only a few seconds passed before they popped back up behind an unsuspecting Malachiel and Terra gave the all clear signal. Visibly pale, Gustavia turned a shaky thumbs up.

Next, Soleil reassured Julie with a grin right before the pair of them dissolved into a beam of sunlight. Seconds later, both reappeared next to Terra. Evian and Kat followed suit by filtering into the finest of cloud-like mists and slowly wafting upward.

"...rule over humans instead of letting their whims and fancies and *free will*," he managed to put air quotes around the term using nothing but the mimicking pitch of his voice, "keep us bound to their service. Higher beings." He scoffed and brushed absently at the Evian cloud as it drifted by at just above eye level.

Adriel's breath caught and held, but she couldn't afford to let him see her attention wander from his face as the little cloud diffused into wisps that threatened to disperse entirely. Left in an expectant silence, she assumed Mal waited for her to comment on his tirade.

Calculating, Adriel burst out with what she hoped would elicit the highest level of response, "Wow, Mal. Who twisted your undies into a knot?" His eyes narrowed at her use of slang, but he got the gist of the question well enough. "You expected an award of some kind?" His dark eyes flashed like lightning, and he whipped his head up to glare down his nose at her. The force of his displeasure added just enough speed to the movement that it created a draft to push the lagging tail of mist toward the rest of the diffuse mass, and in a few moments, Evian and Kat reappeared behind him. Shaken but intact.

Only Estelle and Amethyst were left to navigate the narrow passage between him and the concrete block building beside him. Over one shoulder, Amethyst made a swirling gesture toward Adriel, and her vision abruptly included a clear picture of Mal's aura. A blackened thing shriveled to a husk of withered and wrinkled shadow, it dripped and oozed into the space below his wings. Estelle could easily pass over, but not carrying Amethyst, and going under would mean brushing against the foul essence.

Malachiel continued to vent his anger. "They call themselves sheep, so you can hardly blame me for thinking the same. Herd animals ready to be penned and slaughtered; their souls will feed the darkness when the balance shifts. We'll have our pick of them and not just the culls who exercise their so-called free will to choose the path to true freedom."

Finally, a clue to his motive and it was disturbingly clichéd. History is riddled with stories that illustrate just how fine the balance is between light and dark. Almost every shift happens when someone, or something, tries to subvert free will and alter the definitions of good and evil. Every war, whether human or Fae or demon, has its roots buried in the tiny decisions that tip the scales out of balance in either direction. Nothing in all the words is absolute. Nothing in the human world is ever all dark or all light because that is the only world where free will anchors everything to barely distinguishable shades of gray.

Free will.

Unique to this world, hard to pin down, impossible to predict, and the reason guardian angels exist. Mal was so far off the mark with calling people sheep that it would take a magnifying glass the size of the Hubble to help him find it. Sheep bent to the will of the shepherd's crook was what he saw. In truth, mortals formed the crook, the instrument with which the shepherd herds his flock.

Meanwhile, the final duo of the group gingerly approached the black curtain of Malachiel's aura, looking for a vulnerable spot. Adriel traded barbs with him and watched Estelle gauge her chances of getting through. It was Amethyst who pointed toward the trailing edge of his aura where it ebbed and flowed beside an opening that contained a double door. Each time Malachiel geared himself up for another spate of venomous words, he flexed his shoulders and the shallow opening cleared enough for Amethyst and Estelle to nip inside. If they timed it right, they could wait until another bout of ire cleared the doorway and get past him that way.

Poke him again, Estelle's voice sounded clearly in my head.

Adriel met an exaggerated head nod from Estelle with a slow blink to show she understood what was needed, then attempted to infuriate Malachiel with a well-timed insult.

"How novel, a fallen angel with a Napoleon complex. Are you sure you're up for it, Mal? After all, you washed out of guardianship, so maybe it wasn't about the sheep; maybe you weren't bright enough for the job of shepherd."

She knew she'd been had the second the smirk pulled at his lips. Instead of Adriel stalling him until she could get her people past the perimeter, he had been the one stalling her. Still, his inability to resist posturing led to him folding his arms over his chest, a gesture which perfectly served their purpose. On nimble feet, Amethyst dodged into the alcove and out the other side, hauling Estelle along behind. Malachiel spread his arms wide just as the two passed out of the doorway—just as his aura fell in a shadowed rush behind them.

161

Now it was only Adriel facing the dark angel and trying to decide what to do next. With a backward glance, the others left her there alone. Just as she hoped they would. There were things she wanted to say to the fallen angel.

"Whatever you've done to Julius is nothing compared to what I'll do to you." A truth accompanied by eyes gone cold and bleak. Mal's triumphant smile faltered a little. Regardless of his current status, Mal knew Adriel could not tell a lie. To emphasize her point, she let the light of the universe shine on and through her grace, projecting her true form into the space around her. Overtaking her physical being, the shining, energetic counterpart to his dark beauty rose to a height that matched his.

"The powers won't let you hurt me; I know how those sniveling cowards operate. Forgiveness and love." He spat the words at her. "Weak sentiments. Once we held power in our hands. Do you remember? We pulled the lightning from the sky, played with it like a toy, and sent it crashing to earth again. We built mountains and tore them down just as fast. Until humans came along and turned us into handmaidens while they poured their wishes into the universe." Hate dripped off his tongue to scorch the earth. "We were powerful once, but no more. You won't touch me—they won't let you."

Adriel smiled through the bitterness, "You get a lot of exercise jumping to conclusions like that?"

He sniffed. He actually sniffed; it was downright unmanly. The laugh Adriel couldn't hold back turned into a snarl, and when he opened his mouth to make what she was sure would be another stupid remark, she cut him off without mercy. "Who are you working with, Mal?"

There was as much chance he was in this alone as there was of the sun rising in the west.

162

Malachiel's mouth snapped shut, and she took a step closer. "Come on, you can tell me." she started naming demons and he took a step back. Something akin to fear crossed his face, and she took another step forward.

"You can't hurt me. I know the powers won't let you."

One deep breath, then another calmed and centered Adriel until every last particle of angel rose up inside a body not meant to hold that level of energy, and light shone from every pore as skin and bone and sinew swelled to fit itself to the vision she had already shown. Her truest self.

Galmadriel.

The vision was for Mal's benefit alone, but when asked later, Adriel could swear she heard her brethren singing.

She rose up until she dwarfed Malachiel and he cowered before her.

"The powers don't talk to me these days," her voice fell on him like thunder. "You should ask yourself what that means." She took another step toward him and then one more. Untapped energy fizzled and sparked in her eyes, at her fingertips. Mal looked like he might wet himself.

So, she did what the human side of her yearned to do and, leaning toward him, said in her quietest voice, "Boo."

In a rush of black and cold, Malachiel was gone.

"What a weenie."

Now it was Adriel's turn to nearly pee. She whirled in a blur and saw that girl, what was her name? Alexis, or Lexi something. The one from Evian's house.

"What are you doing here?"

"I followed Evian. I wanted to help. I'm not without a few strengths, you know." Thinking her secret was still safe made Lexi smug.

"Go home, little witch. It's too dangerous for you to be here."

"I'm staying, and there's nothing you can do to stop me—wait, did you call me a witch?"

In Adriel's present state, she thought she could probably lay a finger on the girl and send her back home without even breaking a sweat.

"I did." A flick of Adriel's will lashed against Lexi's resolve which held firm.

"Aren't your kind sworn to smite me? You know that whole *thou shalt not suffer a witch to live* thing?"

Amused, Adriel asked, "Are you a good witch or a bad witch?"

"You've been watching too many movies." Witty banter aside, she needed to get on with her mission and the best way to do that would be to send the younger woman far away.

As if she could read minds, Lexi's eyes narrowed, "Don't even think about it. I may not have inherited my grandmother's evil ways, but I'm still descended from a long line of powerful witches. Who knows what might happen if you try to hurt me." It was sheer bravado, and yet the girl had a point. Plus, now that she was here, Adriel felt duty bound to protect her. Unless…

"Can you cast?"

"We're going fishing?" Lexi frowned and deliberately misread the question.

"Are you or are you not a witch?"

"Oh. No, I can't. The ability to do spells must have skipped a generation." No chagrin colored her tone. Adriel sensed some latent hostility in it, though.

164

Not an asset, Lexi would be a liability and probably safer staying here while Adriel moved deeper into the dark zone.

She opened my mouth to suggest Lexi take cover, then closed it again when the witch's mutinous expression provided ample evidence she had no plans to stay behind, and there was no time for an extended argument. Cautious voices whispered through Evian's shell. The others were somewhere ahead, still shielding and waiting for Adriel to catch up.

"Come on, then. And hurry." Plucking a feather from her left wing, Adriel handed it over. Armed with the best protection available, Lexi fell into step beside the angel, and the two followed the others forward.

Chapter 21

Call it magic, call it chi, call it whatever you want: in those places where world meets world, the stuff of creation rests heavy on the ground, and the laws that usually govern its use don't always hold. Anyone with a modicum of ability can sense a nexus, but it takes more than that to tap into the power contained there.

Intention and will were the forces that had created this particular portal.

Like a galloping horse tasting the wind, Adriel bared her teeth and tuned her senses to sample the strands that made up the portal's walls. Witch, faerie, and the last a total shock—a mythological god. Cupid, to be specific. Some epic event must have occurred to bring this particular grouping together. Then again, this nexus was reputed to be the prison for something called the Darkest Heart, and if you believed the boxes of candy on Valentine's day, hearts were Cupid's specialty.

Adriel, however, knew better. In order to move product, greeting card companies had put quite a spin on the winged one's story. After all, hearts, candy, jewelry, and flowers open wallets. She remembered meeting the trickster god once at a symposium on the emerging technological age. He sat next to her during a lecture on how the wheel would change the world and spent an entire hour making inappropriate suggestions. Hearts and flowers, yeah, right.

Putting that memory aside, Adriel returned to her inspection of the portal. Despite its original make-up, other nuances overlaid it now. Demon-forced cracks spidered the surface, reeked of treachery. To get inside with any sort of stealth would take a person or persons carrying at least three of the founding elements in addition to the more typical combination of a being of light and one of dark, and as far as Adriel knew, between the whole group, they only carried two elements.

She explained the situation to the group. "Lexi, you can represent witch." Turned out to be a lucky thing she had turned up, despite the fury on Terra's face. "Evian can stand in for faerie." It may have been a trick of the light, but Adriel swore she saw Evian's eyes flicker toward Terra, but there was no time to dwell on anything but getting this door open.

"Now, I think our chances of getting Cupid to show up here are about the same as winning fifteen lotteries at the same time without ever buying a ticket, so I'm hoping that given the duality of human nature, the five of us put together" Adriel indicated Julie and the rest, "carry enough darkness. Estelle will bring the light, and between us, it should be enough to pull the trigger." That time she was sure she heard a sigh of relief from Evian and made a mental note to ask her about it later. If there was a later, anyway.

Lexi stepped up to lay hands on the warded wall. Only the mildest tremor of fingers betrayed her show of bravery. Adriel nodded to Evian to go next, but she was busy wiping something out of her eye and gestured for someone else to go ahead. One by one, they all laid hands upon the invisible door. From the outside, it looked like a mime convention. Eye finally clear, Evian slapped a hand into place, and the wall fell away.

They surged through the doorway like weaponless cops. Some ducking low, others staying high. Each team split right or left while Adriel walked straight ahead into the field of battle. Lexi remained behind to hold open the nexus until Leith made his way through—as long as she kept a single hand on the portal, it would remain open, and he couldn't be far behind.

If not for the massive prison enclosure and the unnatural lighting, the inside of the nexus looked pretty much like the outside. Before encroaching darkness had driven away all the people, this area would have been indistinguishable from the rest of the city. The prison took up most of the courtyard of a U-shaped building that had once been home to an insurance company, according to the sign spanning its half-a-block-long face.

Adriel heard Julius seconds before she saw him. Hoarse cries broke from his lips as he struggled against a dark-robed figure. It was hard to see exactly what was happening behind the shifting bars of a prison made from layers of greasy light that pulsed and writhed amid a cloud of acrid smoke.

A second, adjoining cell remained shuttered by a slithering curtain of liquid shadow. Try as she might, Adriel could not see through to what was contained inside.

The full moon glowed like a pearl in the afternoon sky, a vivid reminder of time running out. It was now or never.

"Your friends are going to die, Galmadriel." Malachiel's voice mocked from somewhere ahead and to the left. The choking smoke swirling around the prison walls hid him from view. "And when they do, you'll spend the rest of your life knowing you could have saved them."

"Hey, Mal, why don't you come out where I can see you and say that? Oh, right, I know why, because you're nothing but a puppet and the hand jammed up your backside belongs to a coward." Taunting him was the fastest way to get him to tip his hand. Mal's hot temper often goaded him into acting first and thinking later. That lack of levelheaded thinking had probably been the biggest contributing factor to his downfall, and Adriel knew it would serve her well now.

Silence.

The ploy had failed.

Then a muttered word of power wafted from where Malachiel remained sheltered. Ten yards away, the air tore with a thundering sound. Fire painted the darkness inside the rift with fingers of flickering red, and the putrid odor of ghoul burned Adriel's eyes as the first of a horde shambled through. She allowed the tiniest of smiles to grace her lips. Once again, Mal had lived up—or maybe down--to her expectations.

At least six, by a hurried count, made up the first wave that passed through the shifting slit like some kind of bizarre birthing process. Another half dozen ghouls followed behind the first group as a promise of more to come. As subtly as she could, Adriel channeled energy toward slowing the ghouls until her people had time to take their places.

"Ew, that's nasty." Gustavia's dry understatement nailed it for everyone.

Lexi caught Adriel's attention. Leith was in position, and it was go time.

Fae have a reputation for being bloodthirsty, and while ghouls don't exactly bleed Adriel sensed a thirst in the three sisters for battle. When Evian threw a feral smile over one shoulder, her eyes had gone from the color of whitecaps to the deep blue of an angry sea and were lit with fierce light. With every movement, from the sinuous turn of her head to the measured cadence of her feet, she slid deeper into the skin of the huntress. All three of the sisters moved together with impressive purpose.

Side by side, Evian and Terra worked as a team. A flick of Terra's right hand turned solid concrete to a crumbling

169

mass, and then it was Evian's turn. Twirling her finger in a stirring motion, she pulled water from the air and up from below the surface to concentrate it in the holes Terra had just made. Instant quicksand—and not the painfully slow type. Magic sped up the process and claimed a number of Mal's minions in mere seconds.

One foul-smelling wraith, who was a little smarter than the rest, used the head of a sinking comrade as a springboard and dodged past the sinkholes. Old lucky made a beeline for the two sisters, his bony finger sliding from a dark sleeve to rake Evian's cheek with careless precision. A line of angry red slashed and dripped below her slitted eye.

Seeing her sister take the blow, Terra pointed to the ghoul and screamed an ancient word with the force of a battle cry. The evil thing exploded in a shower of dirt and worms.

"Ew, that's even nastier," Gustavia said.

Evian turned to take on another ghoul while, satisfied her sister was not mortally wounded, Terra stepped over to work with Soleil. Soleil provided the heat while Terra directed it to chosen areas in the paved roads. Heat shimmered over the pavement like mirages, and more minions disappeared into a series of fiery dimples that sealed over them when Soleil reversed her magic to pull the heat back.

While the pair worked their charms together, Evian, shooting off gouts of water behind her, moved to Adriel's side.

"Do you trust me?" The fire in her eyes bored into Adriel's. It was a loaded question needing a fast answer. Adriel couldn't waste time in consideration if they planned to keep Mal's attention focused on the fight and away from the five women who were moving into place to set up a circle of power well within the outer rim of the nexus.

"I guess so."

"Your confidence is overwhelming." Despite the nicks and cuts marking Evian's arms, the glory of the battle showed in every fierce move she made. "Spread your wings, and I'll do the rest."

The rest of what?

Before Adriel could come up with a guess, Evian winked at her and shoved another seashell into her pocket. Water swiftly enclosed the angel's body in what looked like a giant teardrop that left only her wings high and dry. Satisfied with her makeshift weapon, the faerie set the whole thing to spinning like a giant top. With Adriel's wings outstretched, she blasted through ghouls and wraiths leaving a trail of destruction in her wake. Motes of ash drifted in a storm of swirling air currents. And still, the demon-spawn poured into the street. Malachiel had vast numbers on his side, and no conscience to bother him over whether or not his minions stayed alive. It was both an advantage and a disadvantage because ghouls aren't known for being resourceful, and with his attention focused elsewhere, their leader failed to turn them aside from the pitfalls thrown in their way.

In the center of it all, Julius, confined behind bars of light, appeared to be battling against an Earthwalker who was attempting to take him by force. There was no need for Estelle, hovering over the cage and protected from Mal's perception by a complicated faerie charm, to announce the vision of him was all smoke and mirrors. Julius was the bait; Adriel was meant to become the vessel.

I see him. He's okay for the moment. Estelle spoke directly into Adriel's mind.

Then go see to the others. Tell Leith to keep to the plan. We've got this.

Amid smoke and chaos, they played Mal like a Stradivarius. Blood dripped from a few shallow cuts made by

171

ghouls brave or stupid enough to try and force their way past the instant oblivion promised by whirling feathers now filthy and darkened by enemy ashes.

"The circle is ready," Kat's voice rang through the shell network. "Waiting on you for the go-ahead."

Mal's time had come at last. Adriel opened her mouth to give the signal and her moment of gloating came to an abrupt end.

"You lose," Malachiel shouted as he dived through his own doorway and disappeared. Without their leader present, the ghouls lost focus and tried to follow him back through the portal.

"Adriel." The last thing she heard before darkness settled over them like a cloud blocking the sun was Leith's voice. She had almost forgotten he was there, and in the next minute, she forgot again.

The shadow grew deeper, denser yet, and brought with it a sense of hopeless futility. Adriel fell to her knees., her wings fouling when there wasn't time to fold them away. At that moment, all she wanted to do was crawl into the dirt and die. All thought of Julius and the mission to save him faded into a place where life had no purpose or meaning. Despair hollowed her out; made her an empty shell.

The ghouls that had retreated toward the portal surged forward in a fresh wave. Adriel couldn't muster up an ounce of worry for anyone's safety. Nothing mattered; all was lost. Time slowed to a crawl, and she decided this must be what it feels like to live in the underworld.

Hate rolled over her, cast from those in the bowels of hell who no longer cared about balance. Who no longer feared, but welcomed the vacuum of nothingness.

Fulcrum.

The word boomed in her head. It filled her. It stripped her of everything, redefined and rebuilt her from the inside out.

It named her.

Fulcrum.

Adriel had become the point on which everything rested.

Some people see their life flash before them in the moments when death looms near. Instead of the past, Adriel saw her future. Every choice, every possible outcome laid out bare. Some ending in utter darkness, some in light. Still others in the nothing that could come, and with one choice to trigger any of possible futures. She could die right here at the hands of this demon and let the onus pass from her to the one other person now on the face of the earth that could carry it.

Life or death. Hundreds of times that decision would lay before her, and each time the choice would mean as much as it did right now.

Life or death. Yes or no. Help someone or turn away.

We all make choices like this every single day, only for Adriel, each choice would carry the fate of all the rest.

When the red-eyed demon formed in front of her like something built from bits of a child's building blocks, she stared at it in silence. Her ears buzzed, and she recognized a lesser demon standing over her. How did one so powerless as this develop the ability to cause an angel to cower on the ground in quiet desperation?

That one moment of questioning pulled Adriel back from the depths just long enough to trigger the return of sight and sound, and she heard Estelle screaming her name. A pair of booted feet landed in her field of vision. A hand wavered in front of her face, and she remembered him again, not by looks but by something deeper than that—a knowing as deeply embedded as the bones of her body.

Leith, having thrown off the effects of the demon's influence once, thwarted the second attempt to capture his mind the way it had just taken over Adriel's.

With a superhuman effort to choose, she put her hand in his; let each tiny movement pull her away from the sucking whirlpool of hate. In the end, she dropped her hand from his and surged to her feet unaided.

She was the angel Galmadriel it was about time she started acting like it.

Chapter 22

The moment of triumph was cut short by a battle cry from Leith, who stood before the flickering dark form like David in front of Goliath. Unlike David, though, Leith carried no weapon other than the one he had formed from his inner source of power—a seething ball of red energy turned and burned between his hands while he waited for the right moment to use it.

Meanwhile, the demon did nothing but stand there and wait. It was eerie in its stillness, like the calm that lay gentle on the land ahead of a storm, or that moment just before a baby gives forth the first cry. It left everyone feeling poised on the edge and waiting for a push.

Leith looked at Adriel. No, into her—and what she saw in his eyes was so much more than she could have predicted. He might be juvenile in his wit, and too quick with his scorn, but the core of him, the heart, was good and noble and light—albeit with a dark, chewy center. So many contrasts. And they say women are complicated.

There was something else there as well. Leith wasn't planning to walk away from this fight. He would sacrifice himself if need be. Adriel knew what that looked like in a person because it is easy for like to recognize like. Giving her life had become part of the plan since the moment she realized she alone could serve as the fulcrum. The point of balance upon which the darkness and the light now rested. It had all been there in the rainbow paper pattern fluttering against a white wall.

All the way back to the moment when Malachiel had chosen to fall. When Julius had been urged to turn from the light. When Billy's cold finger had touched upon Logan Ellis' corrupted soul. Every moment until now, every step had been meant to lead her here. To the place where she was supposed to give in to darkness and cement the shift.

Even the sticky notes had been a ploy to lead her to this moment. The demon behind it all had known how she would react to the news that upon her choice rested the balance of all the worlds, and had played on that knowledge to set the ring firmly in Adriel's nose and lead her here.

Or so he thought. For, while he might be able to predict Adriel's desire—no, her determination, to save her friends— what he had never seen coming was the way her friends would return the favor. Demons don't look at the world that way.

Adriel made her choice and accepted her place in the world. Fulcrum.

The moment of perfect understanding began to fade just as it must because, despite those rules the angel inside her human body was compelled to follow, Adriel was now a being of free will. Knowing that the fate of the world rested on her decisions was a lot of weight to carry. The moment of perfect clarity had blown through her like a wind, leaving nothing behind to mark its passing.

And she was just Adriel again. Woman. Angel. Adriel.

For one more breath there a relative calm remained, and then the glittering ball of light flew toward the demon's head, and everything went from slow motion to another level of chaos. Estelle and Leith were the only others who remained free of the demon's influence.

"Get Terra," Adriel shouted to Estelle while three long strides took her to Evian's side. A gentle shake brought the water Fae back to herself. One glance took in the entire situation, and Evian's face changed just as quickly as a breeze can stir a lake into ripples and waves. Her features thinned and keened until her cheekbones stood out sharper than a knife edge. Her eyes went dark again as she put her game face back on, and her voice took on the fury of waves crashing against the shore before a storm.

"Finish it," Evian said.

Without looking back, liquid fury stalked past Leith to send a ball of water the size of a Buick toward the ghouls still milling around where the portal had been and scattered them like so many bowling pins. Impotent shrieks rent the air with sharp, whistling blasts that sounded like nails on a chalkboard and made the skin crawl. Worst sound ever.

By then, Estelle had released Terra from the trance-like state and was moving on toward Soleil. Adriel had to trust that Leith could hold off the demon while the preparations for releasing Julius continued. Closing the portal, preferably with big, bad, and ugly on the other side of the door, was the second priority.

Hitting the perimeter where Amethyst, Lexi, and the others should have been, Adriel found undisturbed evidence that the circle was complete, but no sign of the women. Panic shoved her heart into my throat and precious seconds were lost in a frantic search until a glimmer of shifting color revealed the four of them huddled together in a nearby doorway. Amethyst had manipulated their combined auras into a shield that blocked them from sight and sound.

"Hey, come out of there." Adriel tapped Julie on the shoulder since she was the one closest to the mouth of the doorway causing her to jump and let out a little scream.

177

"What was that thing that showed up? It didn't come through the portal."

"Demon." Explanations would take time needed for the ritual. "Salt circle?"

"Got it," Gustavia waved toward a dozen empty containers.

Despite furrowed brows and shaking hands, these women were determined to do whatever it took to free Julius on nothing more than Adriel's say so. She sent up a prayer that she would not let them down.

"Amethyst?" Since much of the burden rested on her shoulders, the aura reader must remain steadfast. "Are you ready?"

"Let's do this."

The four of them moved into position. As soon as Adriel helped get the demon sorted, she would return to give the circle the necessary power.

"What should I do?" Lexi asked. Since she was an uninvited guest on this mission, Adriel ordered her to stay out of the way.

"No. I'm here to help. Find me something to do," she insisted.

"Go over there," Adriel pointed her toward a place where Lexi would be able to see both prison cells and the field of battle beyond. "Stay out of sight and watch that second cage. If you see anything funny going on, you let me know. Can you handle that?"

Lexi grinned like she had a secret. "I can do that. Trust me, you'll know."

It might not be enough to keep her safe, but it was the best Adriel could do, so she returned to the fight, where

Evian's outstretched left hand quivered with the effort of keeping more ghouls from crossing the portal. When a determined one tried to slip past her barrier, she tossed a second ball with her right hand to force it back. "Ha. Picked up the spare. Bowling for minions—the sport of champions."

"How much longer can you hold the door?"

"Just do what you need to do; don't worry about me." Evian's voice sounded harsh with effort. "Help Leith and get on with it."

Soleil and Terra closed the pavement over the head of the last free ghoul, then joined forces with their sister, leaving only Leith to stand against the demon—which was all he seemed to be doing. Standing. Like a statue. Adriel thought she had only been gone a couple of minutes; what had happened to him?

Waving a hand in front of his eyes elicited no response whatsoever. He and the demon were both locked in stasis while the ball of energy continued to burn.

Great. That left two choices: fool around trying to pull Leith out of a catatonic state; or move forward with the plan, and neither addressed the fact that this demon and that ball of energy were both unknown quantities.

Or, there might be another way. A third option that blended the two.

Keeping her voice low, Adriel muttered reassurance as she moved in behind Leith. Close. So close her body was plastered to his. The second their bodies touched, the last of Adriel's latent abilities flared back to life, and Leith's thoughts began a playback loop in her head.

"No good. Less than nothing. Might as well die. Devil's spawn. Waste of flesh. Useless. No good. Less than nothing."

Tell yourself anything long enough, and you will be convinced your statements are nothing short of ultimate truth. Most of us engage in self-defeating inner dialog every day. Leith's mind was filled to overwhelming with phrases turned demon-shaped arrows meant to damage his psyche. Poison tipped barbs to pierce his soul—and the demon still stood without moving. The pair remained locked in silent battle with more at stake than just Julius.

The only sounds now were the muted shrieks of angry ghouls and the harsh whisper of Leith's breath. He trembled.

"I've got you." Adriel opened a connection to Estelle only, explained it would now be up to her to power the circle, sent up a quick prayer for guidance. Running on instinct alone, she held body tight against Leith's back, spread her arms out wide and channeled the white light of creation. A flaring dome slammed around them and hit the ground with shocking force.

That got the demon's attention.

Boy did it ever.

All H-E-double hockey sticks broke loose. The force jarred Evian's aim, which slipped to allow several ghouls past before she regained control. Now on the defensive, the demon forgot about Leith, who dropped out of stasis and shot the energy ball out of reflex.

Despite his size, the demon proved more agile than expected and ducked Leith's red light, which crashed into Adriel's barrier and ricocheted off to turn the escaped ghouls into shrieking funeral pyres. Greasy black smoke that smelled like burning manure and was toxic enough to melt pavement rolled and billowed until the figures finally collapsed into an ashy sludge.

The next minute came in a blur of motion.

Freed from the need for Adriel's stabilizing touch, Leith dodged left and right, throwing another fireball demonward.

Adriel dropped the containment dome. The Earthwalker that had been pretending to assault Julius finally made its move and proved that not only was it too stupid to ever have taken Adriel, it was also too stupid to live.

"Now, Estelle." The response was prompt and elegantly executed. Estelle funneled white light into the ring of salt circling the courtyard until it flared as bright as a miniature sun.

On her nod, each of the four women charged a personal talisman in the ring of angelfire. Julie fed her first camera to the light. When she pulled it back out, it glowed as brightly as the ring itself.

Gustavia had chosen a hunk of quartz crystal as her talisman. Amethyst pulled out a tiny pair of scissors and snipped off a lock of lavender hair to imbue with light. Lastly, Kat pulled a handful of buttons from her pocket to bind to our purpose.

Adriel recognized the buttons as those Kat had once sewn into her clothing to tell her fingers the color of each item during the many years when her eyes refused to see. As symbols went, those bits of colored plastic carried a great deal of power. Combined, the items should be enough to bring down the cage around Julius—and hopefully leave the other cage untouched. No one wanted to be responsible for setting loose a scourge upon the world.

For good or for bad, they were all locked into a confined space with the heart of darkness, a demon, an Earthwalker, and a portal waiting to emit a small army of ghouls.

Who says angels don't know how to have a good time?

Chapter 23

Adriel turned her attention back to the battle and trusted Estelle to handle the prison break. Judging by the fact that Leith's energy balls were looking more pink than red, he wouldn't be able to distract the demon much longer. The Earthwalker circled endlessly and waited for a chance to grab Adriel while the faeries held the portal. All the plates were spinning, but for how much longer Adriel couldn't be sure.

The flare of light when Julius' prison walls went down distracted Adriel just long enough to let the Earthwalker get close. The thing moved in like a bull going for the red cape. Just what Adriel needed to start maneuvering it into position.

Soon enough, Adriel gave the signal, and everything happened like a choreographed ballet.

Like its predecessor, Billy could have told this unfortunate darkspawn, never look an angel in the eye. The walker's gaze swept up to meet twin beams of light and Adriel didn't hold back. There was no vessel to save this time, and so, she hit it like a hammer.

More like a baseball bat. She swings, she scores.

The three faeries jumped out of the way and left off with their assault on the portal. The Earthwalker sailed through the door in a rapidly disintegrating fireball. What was left of it took the rest of the ghouls along for the ride, sucking the rift closed behind it as it went through.

Freed, but still anchored to solid form, Julius stumbled and fell into the waiting arms of his great-granddaughter. Julie wedged herself under one arm, Gustavia under the other, and guided him toward the ring of angelfire where Estelle, in angel form, waited.

Until Julius regained his non-corporeal form, he was stuck here.

Help Amethyst channel the fire into his aura.

On it, Estelle replied. A few seconds passed before she came back with, *Done and safe.*

That only left Kat, Lexi, the faeries, and Leith within the nexus circle. The job was mostly done even if they were well beyond plan B territory. With the pressure lessened, Adriel began to notice something about the demon felt off.

The longer she watched Leith fight it, the odder she found the demon's actions.

You don't live for an eternity doing guardian angel work without running into your fair share of darkspawn, and while this one ticked all the boxes—darkness wrapped around a fire and brimstone interior, the player of seductive or destructive mind games—the passivity it currently displayed was out of character. Way out.

Casting a sense of debilitating dread over someone as powerful as Leith took more than entry level strength, so why, all of a sudden, was the demon playing what amounted to a friendly game of bat the energy ball with the man? Another sizzling orb whizzed past Adriel's ear and set her hair to floating with a static charge. Old red-eye made a show of retaliation but actually lobbed the thing gently toward an unoccupied corner.

Adriel realized later that her next decision set events in motion that would visit dire consequences for some of her crew, but at the time all she felt was a burning desire to figure out why that many ghouls had never gotten close enough to do much more than swipe a claw at anyone.

It made no sense. The faeries kicked butt, but now that they were out of the thick of the fight, something didn't add up.

Skirting Leith, Adriel sought out the three faeries who were checking for stray ghouls. "That went better than I expected." Evian grinned at first, then frowned when she got a look at the angel's expression. "What's wrong?"

"Is it just me or is that demon acting funny?"

"A little, I guess." Evian shrugged. "The bigger question is, what do we do with it now that the portal is closed. Can you send it back?"

As if it had heard her question, the demon roared and focused its attention on Evian. Leith tossed a pallid energy ball, the first and last one he scored on the demon's hide. It bounced off like a slow moving boomerang and took out its thrower who, totally exhausted, had already been on his way down when it hit. Leith hit the ground hard, the demon looming over him, and then Adriel could swear it looked up in dismay.

Her eyes fired, literally, at seeing Leith lying possibly dead at the feet of a demon. *Stupid demon*, she thought, *you're about to go back where you came from with your hair on fire.*

"Adriel, no!" Soleil latched onto Adriel's arm like a limpet, faerie physics lending her a disproportionate amount of force. "Stop. That's not a demon. Adriel, please stop. It's Vaeta. That's my sister. Can't you see she's not trying to hurt us?"

Now, it all made sense. Adriel let the fire cool, but said, "If he's dead, all bets are off." For the span of several heartbeats, everything dropped into slow motion. The only thing unaffected was the flickering curtain of shadow that concealed the second prisoner.

"Vaeta, show yourself," Terra commanded, and the demon shape dissolved, leaving behind the faint shimmering outline of a faerie—a liquid shadow.

"Your man lives." A silvery voice issued from the translucent being of air, "Terra." Her tone was neutral. "Hello sisters. Interesting company you are keeping these days."

Evian arched a skeptical brow, "Hello pot, have you met the black kettle?"

"Touché," Vaeta said with a silken laugh.

"What just happened?" Amethyst joined Adriel at Leith's side to help with his healing. "I feel like I just sat through a long-anticipated movie that didn't live up to the hype." An apt description.

"We've been had." And so had Malachiel, Adriel realized when she played the whole thing back in her head and tried to figure out a motive for the Fae's elaborate ruse. Closing her eyes, Adriel pulled up the memory of the sticky-note rainbow, took a mental step back, and viewed if from a new perspective.

"You've been helping me all along." She interrupted the family squabble. "Playing Mal for a fool so he would tip his hand and expose the bigger plan. You led us here to rescue Julius and made sure I knew I was…" Adriel cut herself off before mentioning the word fulcrum, then continued, "…it was you who attacked Soleil."

"I would never cause lasting harm to my sister; I only needed to get your attention and make certain you would have all the pieces in place when you came to take back your angel. The Reader and her allies were needed. Him, too." Vaeta pointed at Leith. "It all worked out in the end. Think how much you have gained."

"It's nothing compared to what you have lost." Terra's fury burned. "You're dead to me. Do you hear me? Dead. To. Me."

"So nothing has really changed, then?" Vaeta shrugged.

Terra seethed. Soleil, of all people, defended Vaeta. "She was trying to help."

"By nearly killing you."

"It wasn't that bad and if I can forgive her, so can you. Come away with us, Vaeta." The pleading in Soleil's voice made her sister flinch. "Please, we need you."

"You need me? That's rich, coming from the likes of you. Airy Faerie. Airhead Vaeta. Princess Wind Tunnel. Any of those ring a bell? Why would I want to spend another minute with people who would call me such names?"

"It was done out of love." Evian scuffed a toe over the ground like a shamed child caught with her hand in the cookie jar. "We never meant any harm."

Injured pride and underneath that, the deep pain of betrayal. The kind that only comes from those who know you best. Family. Adriel exchanged a sideways glance with Amethyst and left the sisters to duke it out. She could sort out her thoughts on Vaeta's machinations later when there wasn't an injured man at her feet.

"Words carry more poison than a snake can produce venom. But they also have within them the means to heal. Speak your true feelings for your sister, and maybe you will convince her of the honesty in your hearts. Work it out ladies," Adriel advised.

Amethyst laid hands on Leith's prone form, "No serious injury that I can find. He overextended himself and needs to sleep it off someplace safe."

Ignoring the faerie family drama, Adriel checked on the rest of the party and found some minor scrapes and bruises from flying debris, but otherwise, everyone was intact. Once the adrenaline rush wore off, these women were going to need some rest. In the meantime, she turned her attention to Julius.

"I'm sorry, Adriel. I never meant to put anyone in danger." He apologized before she could utter a word of reprimand. "It will never happen again."

Like she believed that. A more impetuous angel might not exist. "See that it doesn't." Adriel's smile belied the severity of her tone. "When this is done, you're to go home, get yourself back to normal, and we'll talk about your punishment later."

Him being safe took a load off Adriel's heart, but she decided they all needed to get out of the reach of the nexus before something worse than a misguided faerie decided to call them out.

Returning to Leith's side, Adriel heard the tail end of a discussion about what to do next.

"We'll make a litter out of that ridiculous cape to carry him out. I saw some old pipes over there," a wave of Lexi's hand indicated the dark prison.

"Stay away from there, young lady. The thing in that cage is more dangerous than you can imagine." The certainty in his voice and the mask of concern on his face as Julius cautioned Lexi caused a twinge of strong emotion. Worry or foreboding, or both. Adriel glanced at Kat and saw the same considerations painted on her face. Despite the anti-climactic ending to this skirmish, the nexus was not safe.

"Show me where. I'll get them." Adriel wanted Lexi to stay right where she was. A sense of unease centered around the young witch was growing.

"They're right over here." As Lexi turned toward the shimmering cage, one last ghoul shot out of the dark recesses of the prison wall and lunged in her face. Startled, Lexi leaped to the side, tripped, and fell heavily to her knees, the momentum carrying her head through the curtain of shadow.

For one split second, it felt like the world might shift. Not much, just a step to the right or left, but enough to change everything. The sensation lasted half a breath before time settled back into place and Adriel realized she was holding her breath.

Nothing happened, except that being closest, Gustavia lunged to grab Lexi by the waist and pull her back to safety while Adriel whipped out a wing and tapped the ghoul on the top of the head. He disintegrated by degrees without taking that sense of unease with him. Lexi sat on the ground with a smear of blood marring her forehead. "I'm okay," she held up a hand when Amethyst moved to kneel beside her, then scrambled back to standing.

"But, please, can we just get out of here?" She looked over her shoulder just once, and a shiver ran down her body.

Julie and Gustavia fetched the pipes and quickly fashioned a stretcher by wrapping the cloak around them and tying off the ends. Good thing Leith's fashion sense included a flair for the dramatic. There was enough cloth to make it work.

As she passed the arguing faeries, Adriel nudged Evian. "Good luck. We're leaving." Evian nodded acknowledgment, then turned back to defending herself against Vaeta's accusations of poor sisterly conduct. The sound of Lexi's attempt to stop the bickering followed the others down the street.

The trip out of the nexus went considerably faster than the trip in. Half a block at most separated the nexus and the verge of Market Street. Julie and Gustavia volunteered to bring the SUV around so they could load Leith in away from prying eyes. In no time, Amethyst turned into the driveway of her tiny house with everyone safe and sound.

For now, at least.

Adriel had a target on her back with the word Fulcrum written in blood across the bullseye. And that was a problem that could wait for another day.

Chapter 24

At seven o'clock in the bloody morning, the ringing of her phone pulled Adriel so thoroughly out of a pleasant dream that she fell off the couch.

Zack didn't even bother with saying hello.

"Adriel, I don't know how you knew, but you were right. Fenton Wallace, AKA Dante, was seen leaving campus on the day of Sylvie's murder. The wit observed Wallace having a heated conversation with, and I'm quoting, *a really big dude* right before he left through the east gate. My gut tells me he's part of it, but there's a problem with the timeline. Half an hour. Even in a fast car, he couldn't get from campus to the alley, kill Sylvie, and get back. He's going to walk because his alibi holds. How did he do it?"

"Malachiel. I found one of his wing feathers in the alley."

"You think he provided the transportation?" There were voices in the background, which meant Zack had to choose his words carefully.

"It's possible. Sylvie swears it wasn't him, but she never saw the face of her attacker. All she saw was the knife, which, from her description, sounds like an athame with a sigil carved into the blade."

A door closed and the background sounds quieted. Even so, Zack lowered his voice so no one would overhear, "I can't get a warrant on a fallen angel, and even if Wallace left campus, his alibi would hold because there just wasn't enough time. He's going to get away with murder."

The growl in his voice indicated how frustrated Zack felt. It wasn't even his case, but getting justice for Sylvie mattered enough that he would spend his free time working the case and feeding information to the investigating team if he thought it would catch her killer.

"There is another way."

A quiet noise in the room pulled Adriel's attention. Leith stood, framed in the bedroom doorway, wearing nothing but the pants she had refused to pull off him when she'd rolled him onto the bed. His eyes still held the slightly confused look of someone just awakened from a deep sleep. Her focus kept returning to the spot where the top button of his pants gaped open.

"Adriel, are you there? Care to elaborate on that cryptic statement?"

"Sorry Zack," She shook her head, but her eyes remained riveted to the man posed so casually in the doorway. "I'm sure you're familiar with the story of Scrooge."

Dead silence transmitted over the phone for a moment and then Zack let out a laugh. "I'll admit it has possibilities. You won't get into trouble with the Powers again, will you?"

"Who do you think gave Dickens the idea for the story in the first place? I'll put something together today and let you know how it goes." Leith's intent gaze messed up her ability to put two sentences together. He had missed the end of yesterday's escapade and deserved to hear how it ended.

"Good morning," Adriel said once she had clicked to end the call from Zack. "Did you sleep well?" The question sounded inane, but nothing better came to mind. "There's coffee, and I could cook some eggs. It's bad coffee. The worst.

Really, you won't want that. Tea? It's Amethyst's place, so I'm sure there's tea. Tons of it, probably." As an angel; you'd think Adriel would have the power over her own tongue. You'd be wrong.

"Bad coffee is better than good tea." Finally, Leith spoke. His voice sounded as rough as the stubble that spread over his chin. It did things to Adriel's insides that didn't slow the flow of words. She jumped up to pour him a cup. To her horror, Leith followed her into the kitchenette in his bare feet. Well, and his bare torso. Too much of him was bare, actually.

"Cream and sugar? Or do you take it black?" The man could rattle her just with his proximity, and the galley kitchen was a small space. Brushing past him to open the cabinet door was an exercise in nearly full body contact. Adriel felt her face flame hot when he made no effort to give her even an inch of personal space.

"How did I get here? You didn't…"

"We used your cape to make a stretcher and carried you out. You know I can't shift between places anymore." Yet. She added to herself.

Leith gave her a strange look—half raised eyebrows, half frown—and before she could ask what it meant, nudged her gently aside, started pulling things out of the refrigerator, and changed the subject.

"Fill me in." He moved around the kitchen like he owned the place. The bad coffee went swirling down the drain, and with an economy of effort, he had the smell of dark nectar wafting through the house. His prowess with the beastly machine Adriel found annoying for no good reason she could name. Maybe that's why she didn't pull the punch when she blurted out the truth.

"The demon wasn't really one of the darkspawn. It was Vaeta, an elemental faerie. Sister to the other three."

A short pause was all that marked the surprise he must have felt. That and the sharp crack of a pair of eggs on the countertop. They hit the sizzling butter and were quickly joined by two more before Leith spoke again.

"That puts a whole new spin on things, don't you think?"

It was a test. Adriel hated tests. What did he see that she hadn't? To buy a little time, she rummaged through the cabinets for the biggest mug she could find and filled it slowly. Cream and sugar killed another few seconds, and then she took a seat at the table.

Everything that had happened over the past few days spun through her mind like an old super eight film reel running at double speed. Meeting Leith, the faeries, Sylvie, Cassandra, Saving Julius—all of it looked different under the filter of hindsight. Good grief, the man was right. The whole thing reeked of hinky.

If Vaeta had never meant to harm anyone, then everything that had happened in the nexus had been a lie. An elaborately wrought farce meant to fool, well that was the ultimate question, wasn't it?

As though Adriel had actually spoken the question out loud, Leith answered, "All of us, to some extent or another, were played for fools." Tension knotted the muscles across his bare shoulders. "You know what this means?"

They spoke together, "This isn't over." Adriel could have told him that before, but until she knew for certain which of the group had been the players and which the playees, the Fulcrum cards would be kept close to the vest. She could admit, though, that it would have been nice to be able to talk about it to someone.

A plate of eggs and toast landed in front of her, and as delicious as they looked and smelled her appetite was gone. When she made no move to eat, Leith tucked a fork into her hand and said, "Don't waste time on brooding. There's nothing we can do about it now, and I want to hear about your plans for putting young Sylvie's killer behind bars. If you let me, I'll help you see her safe. Can I play the ghost of Christmas past?"

His hand lingered on her own a little longer than was necessary, and she didn't pull away. Instead, she met his mischievous smile with a smirk. Did she trust him? Not totally. But she knew that some of the things she had seen in that nexus were true. He was committed to his mission—as willing to lay down his life as quickly as she would put my own on the line.

And if she was wrong, and he had found a way to fool her—well, you know what they say about keeping your enemies close.

***

Sylvie chose a white horse as her means for getting to the other side. Her crossing was something of an anti-climax compared to everything else that had happened that week. Adriel watched her go with a healthy helping of crow in her mouth. Despite all her suspicions, Dante wasn't the guy.

Leith came up with a plan to stage an elaborate bit of theater to pull a confession out of him—theater that bombed harder than the Broadway version of Carrie. Leith barely had time to put on his scariest face when Dante blabbed everything he knew.

His had been the voice Sylvie had heard begging her not to die and cursing his tardy arrival. Malachiel hadn't taken Dante to the alley to kill Sylvie, but to save her. Or that's how Dante saw it. Leith and Adriel agreed that that whole thing smelled strongly of a frame job.

No arrest would be made due to lack of evidence. Dante was convinced that Malachiel had only been trying to help. A pile of black feathers would never convict a fallen angel, and even if it did no mortal prison would have contained him. Dante's alibi held, and Zack was the only police officer who ever learned the real truth.

Satisfied that her lover had been exonerated, Sylvie mounted her white horse, waved goodbye, and faded into the sunset while Adriel wondered how the Powers would classify this assignment. Adding Sylvie's crossing to the balance sheet might put her over into the plus side, but not by much.

Still, Adriel smiled as Sylvie went into the light and rested one hand on the strap of her backpack, hoping that wherever she landed next, she would be a little more prepared.

Epilogue

I am Leith.

The only thing I know for sure is that I was named for Lethe, the Greek spirit of blessed oblivion. Forgetfulness.

Ironic that.

Why? Because I have no memory of my parents, of growing up, of anything that happened before.

Before is a blank slate.

After is a vivid nightmare in blood-washed clarity. Of ghouls and red-eyed demons. Of gentle souls and light.

But not for me.

Never for me.

Made in the USA
Coppell, TX
19 September 2021